'Callum, can't we just. . .forget about what happened two years ago?'

'Yes. Sure. Of course we can, Megan. I hoped you. . .we had,' he replied abruptly.

A steel mask of an expression shuttered his features, and he shifted roughly. Why did he keep doing that? It made her so conscious of his powerful maleness every time those shoulders of his moved in the confines of his shirt. She wanted to lay her head there as she had once done, and feel the slow-burning fire of his passion mounting and mounting. . .

'OK, Callum, I have forgotten. . .' Megan vowed, her voice faltering.

Dear Reader

My starting point was the relationship between Nick
and Helen in FULL RECOVERY. Thinking about
their happy marriage, I started to wonder, What will
come afterwards? Inevitably, circumstances change
and there are challenges. As I wrote, I became
intrigued by the characters of Megan and Karen and
wanted to know what would come afterwards for them,
too. In FULL RECOVERY Karen is swept off her feet
by the wrong man. How does this affect her happiness
later on with the right one? A GIFT FOR HEALING
answers the question. And what about Megan? We
know her in FULL RECOVERY as the Other Woman,
but is it fair to dismiss her that way? Doesn't she
deserve the right man too? I had to find him for her
and then wrote MISLEADING SYMPTOMS to bring
them together. All in all, I felt as much page-turning
curiosity as any reader as this trilogy unfolded.

Lilian Darcy

**MISLEADING SYMPTOMS is the final book of
Lilian Darcy's Camberton Hospital trilogy.**

MISLEADING SYMPTOMS

BY
LILIAN DARCY

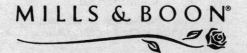

MILLS & BOON®

*First published in Great Britain 1997
Harlequin Mills & Boon Limited,
Eton House, 18-24 Paradise Road, Richmond, Surrey TW9 1SR*

© Lilian Darcy 1997

ISBN 0 263 80121 7

*Set in Times 10 on 11 pt. by
Rowland Phototypesetting Limited
Bury St Edmunds, Suffolk*

03-9705-52757-D

*Printed and bound in Great Britain
by Mackays of Chatham PLC, Chatham*

CHAPTER ONE

'I SEDUCED him,' Megan said simply. There was no point in mincing her words.

'You *what*?' Across the littered dining table Gaye Wyman dropped the leaflet she was folding and it fluttered to rest amongst a pile of its fellows. The older woman's face was etched with a consternation which was almost comical.

'I seduced him, Gaye,' Megan repeated. 'I. . . Well, I can't pretend it was anything else.'

Gaye groaned. 'Callum Priestley! Of all people!'

'I know. . .'

'But, no, Megan, I simply don't believe it can have been like that! How? When?' Then, despairingly, '*Why*?'

Megan put down an envelope and the leaflet she was stuffing into it, her hands suddenly too restless to discipline themselves to the task. She and Gaye were alone in the Wymans' big, casually comfortable house on this Saturday afternoon. They had been at work for an hour or more already, preparing a huge direct mailing to launch Camberton Hospital's new MRI scanner appeal.

Outside cold October rain lashed the windows with miserable persistence and drifts of fallen leaves formed soggy mats on the saturated lawn, but inside Gaye had lit a fire and made hot, milky chocolate to drink: perhaps it was this cosy contrast, coupled with the mindlessness of their task, which had led to the mood of intimacy and female talk—and Megan's shameful confession.

Making light of it and not fooling Gaye for a second, she said, 'I'll answer those questions in the order in which they were put, shall I?'

'Megan, I'm sorry. You don't have to—'

But Megan moved restlessly. 'Please! Now that it's out I'd—I'd like to talk about it, if you could bear to—'

Her voice caught in her throat and her body was bathed in the heat of feverish, relentless memory. That night with Callum. . . She grabbed clumsily at a leaflet and an envelope and began working like an automaton, pretending not to notice Gaye's searching study of her face.

'Of course, if you need to talk,' the other woman said quietly, her face a study in sympathy.

There was a degree of curiosity there, too, which Megan could scarcely blame her for. The one thing that made the whole episode bearable, in hindsight, was that at least *no one* knew of it. Till now, Gaye couldn't have had the slightest inkling. . .

'Um, it's all pretty simple, really,' she began, with a forced, flippant brightness. 'How? We went for a drink together one Friday night after we'd got stuck late at the hospital. We both got. . .just pleasantly tipsy and talked for hours. Or *I* talked. We ended up at his place. I think it was probably the only way he could get me to shut up! When? Two years ago, nearly, in that chaotic period just before Nick Darnell went off to Boston. Why?'

She felt her face burning now. 'If you mean why did he succumb? Because my need was so apparent. I certainly made it very hard for him to turn me down. . .'

'Oh, *Megan!*'

'I know.'

'And yet. . . No, you're wrong, Megan! You must be! Callum is *not* the sort of man who would let himself be manoeuvred or tricked or *embarrassed* into sleeping with a woman if he didn't want to. It can't have been seduction in the cold-blooded sense you mean!'

'No?' She gave me a rather tight little laugh. 'Then please explain why he hasn't spoken to me since!'

'He hasn't? It was a one-night stand, obviously. . .'

'Yes.' She had woken at five the next morning, knowing in bitter hindsight that she had used him, and done a flit. End of story.

'Then obviously it didn't... I mean...the chemistry just mutually...wasn't there,' Gaye suggested.

'No, it wasn't,' Megan agreed huskily—a bare-faced lie.

Oh, God, if only that were true! But, in fact, the slightest nuance of memory of the five hours she had spent in Callum Priestley's bed still, two years on, made her insides roil with a treacherous, unbearable and all-consuming awareness. He still appeared in her dreams constantly, the dark sensation of his hands and lips on her skin so powerful and real that at times it would jolt her violently into wakefulness and she would realise that her whole body throbbed with need and desire for him.

And, still, whenever she encountered him all she could see and all she could think of was his body—moving over her, under her, around her, inside her—bringing her to heights of shared ecstasy and sensation that she had just not believed were possible...

'And yet, surely... He *must* speak to you! He's not the sort of man to—'

'Oh, yes! He speaks to me!' She quoted mercilessly: '"I've scheduled Mr Smith for Monday's list. Mrs Jones's surgery was successful, as we'd hoped, and she's in Recovery. And can I have your opinion on Mr Brown's respiratory status sometime this afternoon?" I suppose you could class that as speaking to me.'

'But perhaps he misunderstood.' Gaye was floundering, although it was nice of her to try to put a good face on the whole thing like this. 'Perhaps he thought—'

Megan finished the sentence for her, the words dragging themselves out, 'Gaye, he thought he'd been used. And I *was* using him.'

'How? Megan, surely not!' Gaye was arguing herself blue in the face now. Funny, really. But Megan's own stand on her behaviour was merciless.

'I was, Gaye. It was all to do with my idiotic infatuation for Nick Darnell. I was such a fool, fancying myself in love with him. Letting myself believe that his marriage was over in all but name, and that if I just played my cards right I could get him to take the final step and leave Helen. Thank God I didn't succeed!'

'I'd have throttled you if you had,' Gaye said energetically, distracted from the issue of Callum for a moment. 'I was so angry with you over that, on Helen's behalf.' Distracted only for a moment. 'But what did Callum have to do with—?'

'I couldn't have broken Nick and Helen apart. I saw that in one blinding flash the moment he told her about their daughter's accident, and I realised what an illusion I'd been chasing and what lengths I'd gone to.'

'You're being far too hard on yourself!'

'No! I won't let myself off the hook like that! I wanted Callum that night to prove to myself that I could do it—find something real—only *it* wasn't real either. I didn't know what I was doing! And to have been like that, to have reached the age of thirty-two without having the slightest idea how to build a genuine relationship with someone. . .'

'Yes, but how could it be otherwise when everything you saw with your parents was so horrible?' Gaye suggested energetically.

In the eighteen months during which their unlikely friendship had been building, Megan had let slip many details about her ghastly family life.

The only child of two people who were bound together by alcohol and shared bitterness alone—who either ignored her or used her as a weapon in their battles with each other—her brains and her ambition had held her to a single-minded course and now, at thirty-four, she was a specialist in thoracic medicine—ready to take the final exams that would give her membership of the Royal College of Physicians. Sometimes, lately, that fact had seemed about as meaningful as a used polystyrene coffee-cup.

It was her groping awareness of the skewed priorities and emotional clumsiness in her past that had led her to seek out family-orientated Gaye as a friend, and the fact that the forty-seven-year-old physiotherapist obviously liked her made her feel—on good days—that perhaps she wasn't quite such an alien life-form after all. Today, though, wasn't a good day.

'I can't go on using my parents as an excuse for ever,' she said now.

'You're not, Megan. *I* did! And you mustn't think there's so very much to "excuse", either!' Gaye threw her leaflets aside once again. They'd never get done at this rate.

'You're a wonderful person! I've seen you emerge like a butterfly from that reserved, awkward little cocoon of yours over the past year and a half. You've always been an excellent doctor. Derek got three letters from patients or their parents just last week, saying how marvellous you'd been during their hospital stays. Competent, caring, explaining everything fully and making sure they understood their choices. Not to mention the fact that you're quite, quite beautiful!'

'Oh, beauty. . .'

'Yes, beauty! You're very, very lovely, Megan, and I'm sure that Callum Priestley isn't any more immune to that than—'

'Oh, Gaye, after all I've said, you're not still hoping. . .?' Because this was how the subject had come up in the first place. Men. And marriage. And matchmaking. Gaye had suggested Callum. 'Do you honestly think he can ever forgive me—for the sake of my looks or anything else?' Catching Gaye's narrowed gaze, alive with the matchmaker's gleam once again, she realised what a betraying question it was and added quickly, 'Even aside from the fact that, well, there was no. . .no spark. No *chemistry*, as you said. He's really rather an ugly man. I—'

'Ugly? Oh, Megan, no! You don't really think so, do you? His face is very rugged, certainly—uncompromising, even fierce at times—but so compelling. Incredibly virile—'

'All right. Not ugly. I didn't mean that. I—I just meant I don't fancy him, that's all,' she insisted flatly, while every pulse in her body clamoured at the lie.

She fancied him horribly! He was her ideal of male beauty now, with his big, almost hulking physique, the ridge of bone that crossed his brow, a face whose planes were so square and craggy they looked as if they'd been hewn with an axe, the starkly green eyes beneath wild, dark hair which felt far softer than it looked, a nose like weathered granite and a square mouth which could kiss like heaven and whisper, 'Megan, oh, Megan. . .' with melting emotion and need. . .

'I'm sorry. I've been pestering, haven't I?' Gaye was saying humbly, when Megan managed to listen again. 'You're right. Who can explain chemistry? Matchmaking is a very bad habit that happily married women on the fringe of menopause are prone to, I'm afraid.'

'Well meant, though?'

'Oh, utterly well meant! But obviously in this case I've picked a lost cause. How about Rob Baxter?'

'No. . . I mean, he's nice but—'

'Or that radiologist with that absurd dog. What's his name?'

'Wooster, I believe.'

'Not the dog, silly girl! Dr Ellis. Peter Ellis, that's right.'

'Peter's nice. Wooster is a nightmare. No, I just can't see myself as Wooster's stepmother, I'm sorry.'

They both giggled, and Gaye began to make ever wilder

suggestions about the romantic possibilities amongst their mutual acquaintances at Camberton Hospital. Then they drifted onto other subjects, leaving Callum Priestley blessedly alone.

'Speaking of the Darnells. . .'

'Yes?' Megan still didn't much enjoy speaking of the Darnells. She had been invited to Massachusetts State University Hospital two years ago, as Nick had been, but had declined the opportunity after all that had happened, and was not sorry about her decision. It would have been impossible for her to go on working with Nick, whose stint at MSUH would probably get renewed for a third year.

He and Helen had a new baby girl now, just a few months old, and she wished the three of them every possible happiness, but she was deeply thankful that they were so far away.

'They're coming back for a break before Christmas, and they've already ordered tickets for this fund-raising ball of ours,' Gaye told her, waving one of the leaflets.

'Oh, good!' Megan managed.

Gaye frowned. 'You mind, don't you, about seeing them again?'

Megan sighed. 'Not exactly. I want to see them again. It's a necessary hurdle and, believe it or not, I've always liked Helen an enormous amount. So, yes, I'll smile and chat and congratulate them on little Therese. But it'll be like taking a large dose of medicine. Unpleasant, but good for me in the end.'

Gaye laughed. 'I won't tell them you said that.'

'Don't!'

As if she knew that she had probed at the subject enough for one day, Gaye began to fold her leaflets in earnest and Megan followed suit until suddenly it was five o'clock. The envelopes were stuffed, stamped and stuck down and the two Wyman girls, Claire and Sarah—aged fifteen and thirteen—trooped in with their father. Both girls were sighing volubly over the young American actor who had starred in the action film they'd just seen, and Megan couldn't resist some mild teasing on the subject.

'Of course, its purely a *physical* attraction,' Claire insisted earnestly, her elfin face a study in pretty blushes. 'I wouldn't ever want to *meet* him, or anything. He'd probably be just *vile* in real life!'

Protesting too much? Thinking of her own protests about Callum to Gaye, Megan suddenly feared that she hadn't been convincing enough. If Gaye suspected. . .

Staying to help make and eat a scratch meal, she seized on a moment of privacy in the kitchen to say desperately, 'Look, I know you probably tell Derek practically everything. . . Would you mind not mentioning Callum Priestley and. . .and. . .you know? It—it wouldn't be fair to him.'

'Of course I won't say anything, Megan.'

'Thanks. It's all. . .completely in the past, after all.'

Apart, that is, from those relentless, tempestuous, torturing memories. Overcome by them yet again, Megan touched her tightened throat, brushed aside a strand of blonde hair which whispered against her face like tender, stroking fingers and then let her hands fall to stir the onions, sizzling in the pan, with quite unnecessary and very absent-minded thoroughness.

Covertly Gaye watched her, a spark of dangerous speculation growing in her light blue eyes.

Megan heard Callum's voice in the corridor of Neonatal Intensive Care well before she saw him and she froze, poised above the tiny baby whose notes she was flipping through. He was on his way to see this patient too. It was there in black and white in the notes.

Little Sally Morgan, born ten weeks prematurely, had developed a cardiac complication, relatively common to early babies, in which the blood vessel connecting the aorta and the pulmonary artery had not closed shortly after birth as it should have done. Patent ductus arteriosus, it was called.

Neither oxygen treatment nor medication had corrected the problem in this case, and now baby Sally risked severe complications if something wasn't done soon. Assessing the infant's blood gases this morning, Megan had not been alone in pressing for surgical intervention.

'I'll tell him you said that!' came Callum's voice outside, and Megan felt her heart begin to beat faster.

She was familiar with the phenomenon. He spoke no louder than anyone else around her although, granted, his uncompromising Newcastle accent was distinctively resonant, and yet it was so often *his* voice which sprang out at her from the middle of someone else's conversation— to set every one of her pulses racing.

She didn't hear a reply to Callum's threat, but now he was speaking again. 'I don't know! The types they let into nursing these days! I think you'd have done better at something else, I do. Had you considered painting very high bridges for a living? Ones that sway a bit in a nice breeze? Being a lion tamer, perhaps, or a rat exterminator? Professional wrestling! Now *that* strikes me as a suitable occupation for someone of your skills and talents. . .'

Now there was laughter from the unseen nurse and seconds later the inevitable happened. He loomed in the doorway of this small room, seeming to fill it with his dark, craggy bulk, and—as if from a distance—Megan heard the high, irritating pipe that was her own, 'Hi, Callum.'

He'd been smiling before—that rough gash of white that opened so suddenly in his face—but now the smile drained away to leave a stiff expression. 'Megan.' His acknowledgement was gruffly reserved—not unfriendly exactly, yet so, so formal—and was accompanied by a little nod which, in a bygone era, would have been a frosty, dignified bow.

'You're here to see this little one as well, I expect?' she said inanely.

'Yes, Baxter wants surgery, too. How are the lungs?'

'Some pulmonary oedema, and she's not doing well off the respirator. I'm glad Rob's decided on surgery. Look at her blood pressure—seventy over twenty.'

'Yes, that's too wide, isn't it? Well, she's first on my list for tomorrow, unless there's a change. Let's have a look. She's still so tiny. It's going to be tricky.'

Tricky? With those big hands it seemed impossible that he could be a cardiothoracic surgeon at all, let alone one who tackled delicate procedures like stitching closed the ductus between the aorta and the pulmonary artery on a tiny infant like this.

Then, of course, she remembered how his hands had moved on her skin that night, his fingers surprisingly long and lean and supple. *That night!* Why wouldn't the memory leave her? Or at least become duller as time passed? It was absurd that she was so aware of him as he stood beside her. *That night.* . . His hands, questing with such delicacy in her most sensitive places, at times quite feverish, at times teasing and unhurried. . . Of course he could perform surgery on infants! His hands were miraculous!

Having to force her concentration, she scribbled something in baby Sally's notes then answered a couple of direct, practical questions from Callum. His questions to her were never anything but direct and practical these days. Sister Tremont, who was in charge of this afternoon shift as well as specialling Sally, came in again and Callum turned to her with some information about prepping the baby for surgery next morning.

Megan used the opportunity to make her escape, then looked at her diary as she hurried out of Neonatal Intensive

Care and realised that she'd be seeing Callum again within minutes as the next patient on her list belonged to both of them as well.

She had to laugh at herself. For two years she'd been playing this game of cat and mouse with him, but to no avail. Inevitably their paths crossed, and would cross again almost daily. Sometimes it was merely a brush-past in car park or corridor, sometimes in a big group of doctors and students on rounds or in case conferences and sometimes, like today, just the two of them at a patient's bedside.

She had no idea how he really felt about it. If in him there was any of the same turmoil that she felt then it didn't show from the outside. He was cool, distant, scrupulously polite. Surely no outsider would ever guess that they had once... And yet Megan herself saw in every line of his figure a hard pride on the subject which told her he hadn't forgiven her.

Why on earth should he? She asked the miserable question for what must have been the thousandth time, and relived it all again. To borrow his own blunt idiom, why the bloody hell *should* he forgive her for what had happened?

It had been a hectic, horrible day, she recalled. With Nick Darnell on leave to prepare for his stint in Boston and the American exchange Fellow who was replacing him not yet on board, she and consultant Tony Glover had had to cover the workload themselves with the help of another registrar and one not especially competent house officer. Inevitably she'd stayed late, knowing that Tony wanted to be with his family at the end of a long week.

Her mind and her emotions had been split into two distinct planes. On one level she'd functioned in her usual competent manner, efficient and focused in the tailored crimson suit which constricted her figure... Yes, she even still remembered what she had been wearing that day!

Because she remembered how he had removed it all later. . .

On another level, though, she had still been struggling with the shame and self-condemnation of the past few weeks—knowing that she'd never really been in love with Nick, and that she'd only been chasing some rainbow goal of tenderness and togetherness—and she had picked Nick to foist her fantasy on purely because he was there, she looked up to him professionally and he embodied the kind of family values of which her own parents had no inkling.

She had started to wonder, too, just how much of it had been due to sexual frustration, to ignorance of her own needs as a woman and to the fact that nothing in her awful family life had taught her the first thing about how to make a relationship.

Fatigue, self-doubt. . . The emotional ground within her had simply been too fertile.

It had been quite by chance that she had met Callum Priestley on her way out of the hospital and evidently he had been tired, too. He'd suggested a drink. . . No, *she* had. . . She couldn't remember!

And yet she remembered the way he had stretched his fatigue-strained neck and shoulders, reaching a hand behind him to massage a burning spot in his spine so that the fabric of his shirt, white in the November darkness, pulled tight across the muscles of his chest and upper arms.

'Nip across to the usual hole?' he'd suggested.

But she'd answered quickly, before she'd thought, 'Isn't there somewhere a bit quieter?' And she had to wonder in hindsight if she'd known even then, in the back of her mind, what she'd needed from him that night.

'Quieter. . .?' he'd echoed.

'If I had to sit in hearing range of a group of exhaustion-crazed housemen. . .!'

'OK, point taken,' he nodded. 'There *is* a place. . .'

And somehow it seemed sensible for them both to go in his car.

The place they ended up at was a folksy pub, and it suited him perfectly. There was a fire, heavy beams overhead, a mellow light and a loose group of folk musicians, singing and playing in the background. In this atmosphere, as always, he looked well grounded, at ease. His strong fingers thrummed on the wooden table top in time to the music, and she commented on them. Their strength. Their surprising sensitivity.

It seemed, in retrospect, far too provocative a remark, but he answered easily enough with a light, throwaway line. He asked her what she wanted to drink and she chose red wine. Potent stuff. Three glasses of it. Or was it four? Much more than she usually had but, still, scarcely a decent excuse. Only she hadn't eaten since breakfast and neither had he so it went to their heads, and after three hours they were still talking.

Did *he* talk much? He must have, surely, because she could remember her fascination with the mobile, ruggedly expressive face and the thoughtful gestures he made with his surgeon's hands. But most of her memory now was of herself—flushed, over-animated, over-intense—telling him the most idiotic things, like how it had felt at university to have her notes on endocrine diseases stolen by a man who'd asked her out twice the previous year.

At some point their hunger was a little assuaged by plates of hot chips, but not enough to stop her head from swimming. Was that how it ended up at midnight, with her lolling on his shoulder while she nuzzled her nose and cheek against that granite face? Was that the origin of her lazy thoughts about how wonderful it felt, and what a rock of a man Callum Priestley was. . .an oaken tree trunk, a fabulous giant of a man. . .? Was that what made her realise that she was going to sleep with him that night—? Hang on! Was *that* when she'd known? Yes, although she doubted whether he'd reached the same decision.

Moments later, though, he was kissing her. Carefully at first, as if he was under a spell—or she was—and he expected it to break. Kissing her hair, her ear, her neck. He smelt deliciously of that morning's aftershave and half a dozen other things. Beer, the wood-smoke from the fire across the room from where they sat, soap, sweat, musk. . . With her eyes closed she lifted her head a little and kissed him back, wanting to taste and explore that stunning, intoxicating combination of scents on Callum's skin.

Within seconds she was drowning in the touch of his mouth, straining upwards to seek out more of him, ready to abandon herself to their exploration of each other there and then—now not caring in the least that the place was almost full and a dozen people might be watching.

He was the first one to pull away, of course. 'Megan. . . Megan, now stop! Stop, OK? You're not fit to—' A helpless groan at her wanton persistence, and another kiss. 'No. . . *Stop!*'

He twisted away and, with vision that was blurred, she remembered now that she had watched the warring feelings in his face. He was as stirred as she was, she soon saw, wanted it as much as she did and she dismissed everything else as unimportant—the searching in his green gaze, the doubt. She wanted him, and he wanted her; wasn't that all that mattered?

It seemed that way then.

'Callum?'

'Yes, Megan?'

'I want to go to your place.'

'Why?'

'You know why.'

'Yes,' he growled. 'I know why. But I'm not sure that I should let you.'

'Why?'

'Because one of us has to have some sense, and it should be me.'

'Are you ac-accusing me of—?'

'Not being sensible? Normally, you're incredibly sensible. Tonight, though. . .I think there's cause for concern.'

'Will you let me be an adult, Callum Priestley? I'm thirty-two years old. Are you saying I'm not cap-capable of taking responsibility for my actions and my decisions?'

'Bloody hell. I know you're. . .' His tight, angry muttering was unintelligible, and just the tone of his voice, burred with sensual awareness, was enough to arouse her. Then he gathered himself together. 'Look, let's give this—'

She didn't let him finish but kissed him shamelessly, feeling his heated male response and lectured him in some garbled way, with her mouth against his, about warmth and intuition and impulse, and in the end. . .

'If you really mean it, then, Megan?' he said in that low voice which seemed to have incredible power that night to do something very strange and seductive to her insides.

'Yes. Yes, of course I do.'

'This isn't the way I thought—'

'So? Does it matter?' she demanded.

'Doesn't, I suppose.' Opalescent fire shone in his green eyes; she sensed a holding back in the line of his mouth and his shoulders. The fire won out. 'All right.' Another searing kiss. 'Let's go to my place.'

She kissed him back and heard his groaned, 'God, Megan. Bloody hell, Megan. . .' muffled against her mouth and hair.

And that was the last thing she remembered clearly for the next five hours. His place, a pleasant little one-bedroomed flat, was literally just around the corner and she was afraid that those beers must have gone to his head even more than the wine had gone to hers, because his control of the vehicle slipped twice. He kangaroo-hopped

as he started out of the pub's car park, then in his own
outdoor parking spot below his flat he rammed the kerb
hard with his front tyres, before braking adequately.

His laugh, as he switched off the engine, was shaky for
some reason and his words ambiguous. 'Sorry. . . I wasn't
prepared for the pace!'

But he was. In bed, oh, he was! She hadn't known what
to do once they got inside, other than to pitch herself
immediately into his arms. She must have been so
awkward!

She struggled with her jacket, kicked off her shoes and
started looking for the zip on her skirt until he stopped
her, almost imploring her—if she remembered this
rightly—not to be in such a rush. And he took over the
whole thing—the pace, the atmosphere—with a masterful
tenderness, a caring control and ultimately a passion that
left her. . .

Oh! It washed over her again and she had to stop in
the corridor outside the paediatric medical ward to gather
herself and still her trembling.

In his big bed, feeling his feverish gentleness as he
peeled away her clothes, bathing her with kisses, saying
her name. . . Darkness, apart from the light he'd left on
in the tiny hall which spread one fuzzy golden finger
through the open bedroom door. . . His hands, holding her
as if he could never get enough. . . Her own wonder at
the perfect feel of him—his heavy, honed muscles, the
hair that defined the shape of his chest, fuzzed his forearms
and made a fine, silken patch in the small of his back, his
hard male nipples, flat navel and steel thighs.

And then the way her body seemed to be in the grip of
some flood-tide, carrying her along and sweeping her out
to a dark sea of sheer sensation. Her head pillowed against
the broad bulwark of his chest. Her fingers feeling his
face as if she were blind. To a blind person his face would
feel quite perfect, she decided hungrily—so strong and

meaningful and well defined—and she had kissed every rough-hewn plane.

Callum. Callum. She didn't dare to trespass too far into the memory of the moments when they had joined together fully. The weight of him, his certainty, his abandonment. Their cries, their incredible hunger and, finally, its satisfaction.

To lie sheltered against his warmth and his bulk, feeling his breathing, blanketed by his protective touch as she felt both of them slip into sleep was the safest, softest feeling she had ever known. When she woke a little later, to feel him caressing the full weight of her breasts and sliding his hands down the scooping curve that ran from her ribs to her hips and slipping across between her thighs, she wanted him again; gave herself to their passion again, with an intensity that left her face wet with tears.

'Ah, Megan,' he crooned. 'Don't. . . Don't. . . I knew I shouldn't have. . .'

'Yes. . . Yes, you should!'

'I didn't hurt you?'

'No, Callum.'

'Because I'm so much bigger than you. . . If I crushed you. . .'

'No!' She didn't want him to talk so she kissed him into silence and they lay there again, with her head pillowed on his chest once more, and she heard him murmur with the sleepy shred of a laugh in his voice, 'Incredible. . . Little did I think. . .' before they both drifted into sleep once more.

Her next awakening, two hours later, was very different. The alcohol must have left her system, taking with it the soft-edged, giddy happiness—the hazy feeling that she'd arrived at some wonderful place that she didn't have to leave ever again if she didn't want to. Instead she was left dry in the mouth, headachy, and gloomed over by the low ebb of the small hours when nothing ever looked rosy.

She was reminded of her parents and their drinking—the euphoric plans and extravagant declarations made during the first gin and tonic when they arrived home in the evenings, the sodden stupor that descended after the third bottle of red wine and the hair-of-the-dog tot of whisky over breakfast the next morning when both of them smelled and scowled and didn't want to go to work. . .

Callum was still sound asleep, his peaceful face a primitive mask, softened only by the faint smile that floated on his lips. Suddenly he seemed like a stranger, and the sounds outside his flat, the light and shadow and the clean smell of the place were strange and unfamiliar too.

With an almost physical rush of regret, she rebelled against the seductive pleasuring of her body and thought, What am I doing here? What on earth am I doing here with a man I barely know, when just a few weeks ago I could make such a hideous mistake over Nick Darnell? Isn't this still a part of that? Just as wrong, just as misguided?

Looking at Callum, she was afraid of him. He looked so powerful, still naked, flung out beneath the tangled sheet which did nothing at all to hide the flagrantly male sculpting of his shape. He seemed like some ancient god from Greece or Rome—elemental, physical, and capable of great anger and retribution.

Her heart pounding, she untangled herself from him with painful slowness and care—irrationally frightened of what he would do if he woke up and caught her at it. But he didn't wake: not as she eased out of the bed; not as she dressed again in the underclothes and suit which lay crumpled on the floor; not as she crept out of his flat with her crimson shoes in her hand and closed the door behind her.

Five o'clock in the morning. No taxis. It was only as she walked the streets in search of a phone-box to ring for one that she realised that here was where the real danger lay—in the dark of the deserted city at night. Why had she been so frightened of Callum who had shown her nothing but gentleness and care even at the height of his physical abandonment?

It was her own conscience, she knew suddenly, clamouring against the new conviction that she had used him to prove something, or to forget or to pretend to herself that she knew what she wanted.

Did Callum understand the truth as well? That she was on the rebound from a shallow infatuation and might equally well have ended up in bed with. . . Well, who? Rob Baxter, perhaps, since he was currently unattached and she liked him. Others? Which others?

As the taxi delivered her home she thought blackly, I'll never know, will I, just how low I might have sunk last night? I was very lucky that it happened to be Callum!

Incredibly lucky! And there had been a part of her—barely acknowledged—that had waited eagerly for him to ring, or say something at work or find an opportunity to kiss her again. The wait hadn't lasted long. She was so aware of him that she could barely even greet him the next twice they met, and it had taken her perhaps a week to detect the impenetrable distance beneath the black armour of his reserve, his dignity and his rather blunt professionalism.

He knows, was her stark, miserable conclusion. He knows I was using him, and of course he can't forgive it. Why on earth should he?

Two years had passed since then, and that scrupulous armour of polite distance remained. It didn't seem likely that his attitude would ever change. And, of course, she couldn't blame him in the least. If it wasn't for the way her body remembered his so insistently she might have been able to chalk the whole thing up to bitter experience. As it was, Callum Priestley remained a very disturbing thorn in her side at least half a dozen times a week and she regretted her heart-to-heart with Gaye on the weekend, which only seemed to have rekindled the issue in her mind.

Pulling ineffectually at her clothes, as if their constriction was the problem, Megan controlled her runaway memories and entered the children's medical ward.

CHAPTER TWO

CALLUM observed Megan Stone's carefully unobtrusive departure from Neonatal Intensive Care, stoically unsurprised. By focusing on Sister Tremont he'd deliberately helped his medical colleague to make a getaway that wouldn't confront either of them with the embarrassing and difficult need for further polite, meaningless talk.

After a few more minutes, which would ensure that Megan was well on her way to the paediatric ward and thus obviate any possibility of their having to make the journey together, he planned to depart as well. First, though, creating an additional useful delay, he had another tiny patient to see here in NICU—post-operative and recovering nicely, despite a weight which still hovered at just under two kilograms.

He stood for a minute, collecting his thoughts, as he watched Jason Wheedon's ribcage expand and contract with each miraculous breath.

There was an almighty audacity, he sometimes considered, in his even attempting surgery on such tiny babies and yet he did it, with a quiet arrogance essential to his profession, and wonderfully often they survived and flourished when once they would have certainly died— with surgery or without. It was intensely satisfying. . .

This little bloke. . . He examined the still raw-looking incision, checked flow sheets and gave the baby that almost intuitive few moments of scrutiny which sometimes picked up warning signals that all the monitors in the world couldn't measure. Today, though, blessedly, there was nothing to worry about.

Which gave his rather distracted mind licence to think

about Megan Stone, although there was nothing new for his brain to process on the subject. As usual, she hadn't met his eye as they talked. As usual, she had seemed so uncomfortable in his presence that he might have been justified in wondering if he'd left some vital part of his clothing unfastened or come in to work with an egg moustache from breakfast still encrusted on his upper lip.

But, of course, it wasn't that. Two years ago, in a night of passion the memory of which still made his skin crawl and his loins ache with desire, he had taken terrible advantage of her vulnerability. She still hadn't forgiven him for it, and he wasn't in the least bit surprised.

I knew the whole evening that it would be wrong of me, he mused. After the wine, her vulnerability cried out at me. . . Only she made it so bloody hard, so *impossible*, to say no!

No, he corrected himself firmly as he left the NICU, he couldn't take that cop-out. Yes, she had laid her head on his shoulder but he was the one who had turned her face to meet his kiss and, God, he couldn't blame *her* for what she did to him physically! It wasn't as if she'd just switched it on that night, after all.

He'd fancied her from the beginning, sweltered with it, and his quiet knowledge in the weeks before that night that recently she had been caught up in a hopeless love for her married senior, Nick Darnell, hadn't done anything to make the heat in him subside.

Something must have happened, he had realised that night. They must have had a confrontation. Or perhaps Helen warned her off. Somehow she's over it, but she's a mess and she needs to be talked to. . .touched. . .held.

But he should never, never have let it go as far as it did, not when she'd had that wine and not when she didn't really know why she was doing it. It had been easy to conclude this in the cold light of the following day when he had woken, sated with sleep and sex, to find her gone from his bed. The night before—the way their bodies had played on each other, sung to each other, miraculously tuned—had seemed to suggest a *rightness* to the whole thing that overrode the terrible timing of it, the emotional imbalance between them.

'But bodies lie,' he muttered now as he headed up to the paediatric ward. 'Bloody hell, do they lie!'

He should never have believed his treacherous senses, let alone the arrogant voice inside him which had insisted that one night in his bed would dissolve any possible problems. He should have known!

Because reality had set in with a vengeance after that heady, miraculous night. He'd wanted to phone her at once; suggest. . .a *date*? It had sounded so insipid after all that passion—the idea of a genteel little meal somewhere. So he had held off for a crucial couple of days, during which time he'd seen her at work and one look at her face had confirmed the foreboding message of his cold morning-after bed.

She'd realised what an opportunist he had been to accept her willing body, and now she hated him for it. He didn't blame her in the least.

For quite some time after that his whole body had burned with a painfully physical regret, but then the inner vein of self-sufficiency which had got him through a pretty brutal working-class childhood and some gruelling years of study to bring him to his present position of Consultant Cardiothoracic Surgeon at Camberton Hospital had asserted itself and he'd schooled his need away.

With the mess his parents had made of their marriage and the memory of his well-bred university girlfriend's final pronouncement on their romance—yes, it still stayed with him and rang in his ears now, 'Nothing personal, Callum, but you're not exactly blessed with the sort of gene pool one wants to *blend* with,' —he had to conclude that he was more fitted to the life of a lone wolf in any case.

So be it. He would make a success of it in his own uncompromisingly individual way, and if Megan Stone could still set his blood on fire with her—

'Damn!' he drew a ragged breath and had the illusion that he could still smell her on his skin. 'It's like malaria! There's no cure!'

Bhasa Singh was a very sick little girl, and Megan now knew her better than any doctor ever hoped to know a young patient. Bhasa was so familiar with this hospital and its routines—the casualty department, paediatric intensive care and this, more benign medical unit—that she had confounded young house officers more than once in the past by knowing more about her illness than they did. And she was still only six years old. . .

Diagnosed with asthma before the age of twelve months, she was a chronic and acute sufferer and it had taken years to understand what brought on her attacks and which combination of drugs best controlled those attacks or kept them at bay.

Until recently her mother, Nimiksha, had been outstandingly conscientious about keeping the house clean, well humidified and free of all irritants, keeping a journal about Bhasa's health and activities so that patterns and triggers could be more easily identified and doing a dozen other things that helped—though not always—to keep down the severity and frequency of Bhasa's attacks.

Nonetheless, even during those early years there had been many hospitalisations and Bhasa's small trachea had been breached twice by emergency surgery to ease her breathing.

And now Mrs Singh was pregnant, having delayed trying to conceive a second child for several years as she and her husband focused on caring for Bhasa. Now, in her ninth month, the pregnancy was taking its toll on her energy levels and she just wasn't able to maintain quite the same standards as she had done previously. Undoubtedly Bhasa was feeling anxious about the changes a new sibling would make, too, so it was for a complex mixture of physical and emotional reasons that her attacks had got out of control several times over the last few months.

Having dealt with Bhasa's asthma for two years, since taking over from Nick Darnell as the little girl's specialist, Megan had at first felt confident that her asthma could be brought under better control as she emerged from the toddler years, but the condition had confounded her best efforts. Two weeks previously, with tests of blood gases showing anomalous results, Megan had suddenly wondered if there could be an unrelated and previously undetected heart problem at work in small Bhasa.

There was. It was a fairly rare congenital abnormality in the mechanism of the heart, which would almost certainly become more serious as the years passed but which could be corrected by surgery.

Which was where Callum Priestley came in, of course. The operation was scheduled for two days hence.

'How are you feeling, Bhasa?' Megan asked, coming up to the high white bed in this four-bed section of Children's Medical. For the moment the other beds were unoccupied as the other three small patients were still elsewhere in the hospital, having physiotherapy or tests.

Bhasa just wrinkled her nose and Mrs Singh, looking huge and very tired, smiled faintly and said, 'Not such a good day, I'm afraid, Dr Stone. She didn't want to take her medicines and got herself all upset and wheezy.'

'I did take them,' Bhasa said, breathily indignant as she lay propped up against her pillows. The sheer work of breathing exhausted her after only short sentences. She was small for her age, and Megan wondered—a nagging, pointless question that she'd asked herself since the heart diagnosis was made—If she hadn't had asthma, would we have thought of a cardiac abnormality sooner? Did it blind

us to the symptoms? And is surgery now the right answer?
It's risky. . .

'You did take it in the end,' Bhasa's mother was saying,
'but I had to promise you all sorts of treats after the
operation, didn't I?'

'It's not fair having to take *extra* medicine.' Since
Bhasa's asthma was so intractable she was on a carefully
managed regime of corticosteroids, which suppressed the
function of the adrenal gland. This meant that during the
physical stress of surgery the natural boost of the body's
steroids—normally produced by the gland—would be
missing and had to be supplemented artificially, starting
two days before the operation was to take place.

With her life measured in doses of numerous different
drugs, it wasn't surprising that Bhasa rebelled against yet
another one.

Megan patted her small shoulder, wishing that there was
more she could do, and touched Mrs Singh as well. She
really did look exhausted. They both did, although Bhasa's
admission to hospital three days earlier had been designed
to help both of them gain strength and rest before the
stressful surgery.

'Mr Priestley should be here very soon,' Megan said.
'He's the surgeon who is going to be in charge tomorrow.
Have you met him yet?'

'No,' Mrs Singh said with a frown, 'I don't think so.'

'You wouldn't forget this man if you had,' Megan
blurted out, then wished she hadn't and back-pedalled,
making it worse. 'He's. . .um. . .fairly distinctive.'

'We've met his registrar. She seems nice.' Mrs Singh
had noticed nothing odd.

'Yes, that would be Ariadne Demopoulos,' Megan said.
'I only know her by sight. She'll be assisting, I expect.'

'Does it complicate the surgery itself—the fact that her
asthma is so bad?'

Megan was careful this time in what she said. 'It can.

It takes extra care. Do you know who the anaesthetist will be?'

'No. I might have been told, but I can't remember. There's so *much* to remember!'

'I know. Well, let's see, it'll probably be either Ron Rose or Andrew McCarthy, and they're both extremely skilled and very aware of what Bhasa's condition will mean.'

'Will *you* be there, Dr Stoney-stone?' Bhasa's little voice piped up, and her thin hand snaked up to pluck at the cotton sleeve of Megan's coat. She had a broad Yorkshire accent, in contrast to her mother's richer and more fluid tones.

Megan hesitated, although Bhasa's tender nickname and little gesture had twisted her heart. She could be present in Theatre on Friday. She had considered it. . .until she had realised that Callum would be the surgeon in question.

'I—I don't know, love,' she said. 'I'd like to but—'

'Dr Stone has lots of patients to look after, not just you, Bhasa,' Mrs Singh interposed, although an eager flicker from her dark eyes told Megan that she, too, would like the presence of a familiar doctor during surgery.

'As sick as me?' It was sometimes a source of odd, heart-rending pride to Bhasa that her asthma was so intractable.

'Actually, yes, I'm afraid so. Some of the big people I look after are *quite* sick,' Megan said.

She was on the point of adding, though—thrusting personal qualms aside—that she *would* be there on Friday but then she saw Callum in the doorway and had to struggle against her usual response to that dark bulk. He'd have seen Bhasa's notes and heard his registrar's report, and that of the cardiologist, but that wasn't enough and Megan knew that he'd want to talk to her in more detail about Bhasa's asthma after this meeting with the patient herself. She wasn't looking forward to it.

'Is this Dr Priestley?' Mrs Singh murmured, and Megan was too caught up in her usual struggle for poise and control to correct the erroneous title of 'Doctor'.

'Yes, it is.' Then, as he approached the bedside, Megan said, 'Callum, this is Mrs—'

But suddenly Bhasa was in tears, positively bellowing with fright, and all three adults could only turn to her in consternation. She was wheezing almost at once, her words quite unintelligible, and she had to be given a dose from her inhaler before she was at all coherent or in control. It took time and Megan was aware of Callum, standing behind her and waiting. She felt flustered and unable to reassure Mrs Singh, who was wringing her hands. What on earth had gone wrong so suddenly?

Then Bhasa said, with sobs still threatening, 'I don't want him. I don't want Dr Beastly!' and out of the chaos and hysteria there was a sudden embarrassed silence from the adults.

'Not Dr Beastly, darling, Dr Priestley,' Mrs Singh said, but in her accent there wasn't a lot of difference between the two and Callum's rugged features *had* looked rather fierce as he entered, his jaw set and his heavy brows lowered—as if he had been wrestling with some recalcitrant problem that he couldn't immediately dismiss from his mind.

Bhasa roared in wheezy terror again and Megan bent towards her then straightened again, totally at a loss as to the right thing to say. It was awful! Daring to turn to Callum, she expected to find him furious or deeply embarrassed but he looked quite placid and calm and then, all of a sudden, he smiled. It broke across his face like a strong shaft of sunlight on crystal-veined rock, bringing an immediate warmth and a twinkling-eyed softness that couldn't be other than utterly genuine.

'Would you like to call me Callum, then?' he said. His

voice had a cheerful, matter-of-fact lilt. 'I like my name—Callum. It's Scottish.'

'Callum,' Bhasa echoed, smiling back at him. 'Like calamine lotion. Dr Calamine.' She studied him carefully for a moment, then reached a decision. 'You're not beastly at all, really, are you?' Then, in a very audible aside, she added, 'Mam, you must have got it wrong, you must. He's not Dr Beastly; he's Dr Calamine and he's going to be nice.'

The three adults exchanged covert smiles over the little girl's head, and Megan marvelled as she conceded her relief. It could all have been considerably embarrassing, yet Callum had calmly carried on and now, instead of a terrified little girl and a surgeon irate at the compromise of his dignity, the atmosphere could not have been more relaxed.

'Dr Calamine' brought out a plastic model of the human heart with detachable sections, and Megan stood back and listened while he gave a serious, simple and incredibly reassuring explanation of exactly what he was going to do on Friday and exactly how it would help Bhasa. Despite the frequent illness and absence which had held her back at school, Bhasa was a bright little girl and she listened intently to every word. She even had a question at the end.

'Will you have to go inside my chest again to take out the stitches?'

'No, I'm going to use special stitches which dissolve all by themselves,' Callum said.

Mrs Singh had been listening to all this as well, and she interjected, 'Dr Stone thinks she might be able to be present.'

Callum turned to her with a question on his face and, put on the spot, Megan had to put her personal reluctance aside. 'I'd like to,' she told him, 'if that's all right.'

'Of course it is. And I'm sure Ron would appreciate your input.'

'Oh, it's Ron, is it? I wasn't sure. I talked to him about anaesthetic agents and IV aminophylline when I was sorting out the boost of steroids, but he said it might be Andrew actually in Theatre.'

'No, it's Ron. Can we talk later?'

'Yes, I thought you'd want to,' she nodded, hiding her reluctance as she knew he was. The last thing the Singh family needed was to be aware of personal tensions between members of their daughter's medical team.

'My office?' Callum suggested. 'I've got appointments from four until six.'

'Same here. So six would be good,' she told him, her breathing shallow and unsteady.

It was almost four now, and they'd both sandwiched some time before their scheduled office hours to come and see hospital patients. Megan decided that *next* time she shared a case with Callum she'd visit the patient straight after lunch. . .which was a pointless plan, since sharing a case inevitably meant having to consult with one another over it. She'd been living with these meetings for two years now. She could go on living with them.

So. . . Six o'clock in his office. She took her leave of Bhasa and her mother, being quietly authoritative on the issue of both of them getting as much rest as they could between now and Friday, then went up to the cystic fibrosis section of the paediatric ward to see another patient whom she had known for some time. For four years, in fact, since she had first arrived at Camberton. Fortunately this time Callum wasn't involved.

Gary Henley resented being hospitalised in the paediatric ward these days. He was nineteen, and prone to the spurts of rebellion that were common to all adolescents but which provided added problems for CF sufferers. His illness, genetic in origin and as yet incurable, had already had countless ups and downs over the years.

That afternoon, when Megan entered, he lay there

sulky and listless, connected to oxygen, a drip and the gastrostomy tube he used at home as well—which enabled night feeding of high calorie and energy nutrients directly into his stomach while he slept.

His response to her cheerful, 'Hi, Gary,' was only a grunt. Then he sighed and, with an effort, pulled himself higher in the bed.

'Sorry, Dr Stone. . .'

'What for?'

'For scowling.'

'You don't look very comfortable. Is there anything I can do?'

'I hate this gastrostomy tube. . . Oh, and my drip got pulled out accidentally half an hour ago, and that Dr *Death* who put it back in—'

'Dr *Death*?'

'All right, Dr Tompkins, then. I can't stand her, and I almost refused to let her do it. Wish I had! I would have done if I'd known you were coming so soon. It took her four tries before she got a vein and she got more upset and nervous every time, though she pretended she wasn't. Just like Mum when she used to be scared of my Kangaroo pump.' This was the device used at home to deliver his night feeds. 'I could have done it better myself!'

'I'll have a talk to her,' Megan promised, preparing for a longer stay at Gary's bedside than she had allowed for.

Gary's parents were divorced, and his yearning for a male role model was very apparent at times. He had scant patience with anyone who didn't treat him with brisk energy and confidence, and reacted particularly badly to what he perceived as feminine fussing. . . Although at the same time he had quite a way with the girls and had several female CF teenagers at his clinic in a bit of a state over his fine-boned and compact good looks.

'Anyway, the drip's not important. It's in now,' he said.

'But the tube. . . Can't I have a softer one? This isn't the same kind I usually have.'

Megan nodded frankly. 'I know. We were hoping it wouldn't matter with you in bed most of the time. But it's uncomfortable, is it?'

'You could say that!'

'The softer tubes are on order. We'll change it as soon as we can.'

'Why didn't you tell me? Don't treat me like a kid! Don't *protect* me! If I'm told what's going on I can handle it.'

'You were feeling pretty low the day we replaced your old tube, Gary,' she reminded him.

He nodded. 'All right, so I'm just being a pain.'

'You're not, and we'll change the tube and I'm sorry I didn't tell you what was going on. Now. . .'

She put her stethoscope to her ears and had a good listen to each lobe of his lungs as he breathed for her. Despite the vigilance of Gary and his mother, as well as the CF clinic staff, he'd caught a chest infection and been admitted last week, just at a time when his gastrostomy tube had once again worn thin and needed replacement. The infection was clearing, but it was a slow process and, meanwhile, Gary was losing much of the fitness he'd worked so hard to gain.

His cystic fibrosis had been diagnosed at birth when his lower intestine had been blocked by the characteristically thick meconium of CF babies, and when the jaundice common to many newborns had persisted for much longer than usual.

Since then the lifespan he could hope for had increased year by year in response to the dramatic advances in treatment of the disease, but setbacks still happened and, ultimately, deterioration was inevitable. At some point in his future he would probably need to be sent down to a more specialised hospital in London, and a heart-lung transplant was on the cards within the next ten years as well.

'When do you think I'll be home again?' he wanted to know and Megan was able to tell him, after looking at his chart, 'By the end of the weekend, I should think.'

'Brill! OK, I forgive you lot for the tube, then.' He looked towards the doorway, considerably more cheerful now, and greeted the woman who had just entered. 'Hi, Carol. You've got that elegant outfit on again, I see.'

'Are you flirting with me, Gary?' laughed the physiotherapist as she put her clipboard at the foot of the bed.

'Course I am! It's very sexy, having a woman come and pound the stuffing out of my lungs several times a day.'

'Don't get too cheeky, sir,' Megan cautioned him, 'or she might pound a bit harder than you need.'

'I won't, Gary,' Carol Bernard said. 'I'm au fait with his particular brand of repartee, Dr Stone, don't worry.'

'Well, I'll leave the two of you alone, then.'

'My tube, Dr Stone. . .'

'I won't forget, don't worry.'

Megan left, hearing Carol's comfortable voice as she helped Gary into position and then the rhythmic sound of hands working to loosen the thick secretions in his chest.

Back in her office, she plunged into her office appointments with such fierce concentration and conscientiousness that she inevitably ran late and it was a quarter past six when she finally hurried up the stairs and along the corridor to the opposite end of the doctors' building, where a bland black-lettered sign on a bland wooden door announced, MR CALLUM J. PRIESTLEY, MA, FRCS. CONSULTANT CARDIOTHORACIC SURGEON.

He must have run late as well. Megan met an elderly gentleman and his wife, fussing at each other along the corridor, and when she knocked the door was opened by Callum's secretary, who was just tidying the outer office — ready to leave.

'The coffee's on,' Cecily Stark said, tying a patterned silk scarf over her greying hair.

'Thanks, but—'

'I know Mr Priestley wanted one. He's just finishing some notes, if you'll wait.'

'All right, I will have coffee, then and I'll get his, too.'

'You know where the kitchen is.' It wasn't a question, and it was rather stiff and cool.

She doesn't like me, Megan thought. She definitely doesn't like me.

Having met Mrs Stark numerous times before, it wasn't the first time that she had received this impression. Needless to say, it wasn't pleasant and she wondered wearily what the origin was of the older woman's harsh assessment of her. She went back down the corridor to make the coffee, and realised that she didn't know if Callum took milk or sugar. It was one of the million and one things she *didn't* know about the man she had slept with. Should she ask Cecily Stark?

But she heard the echo of sturdy heels and then the sound of the door to the stairs. Mrs Stark had gone. She left both coffees black and unsweetened and went back to the office where Callum's inner door was now open, although he was still scribbling at his desk.

Looking up, he gave a distant nod then saw the coffees and sat up more eagerly. 'Ah! Life is worth living after all!'

'I hope it is.'

'What, no milk left?'

'Yes, but I didn't know that's what you took,' she answered. 'I can get it. And sugar, too, if—'

'Don't be silly!' He went to get the milk himself and, alone in his office, Megan waited stiffly, wishing that the meeting was over. . .

But she had to stop to wonder just why she found it so terrible. Callum could have made meetings like this very hard for her, but he never did. He was cool, true, but he could have been a lot colder. Really, it was only his scrupulous professionalism which had made it possible for them to keep meeting at all after what had happened two years ago. She ought to be grateful and follow his lead. In fact, she tried to but her body's response to him let her down every time. No more of it! Forget it!

But how. . .?

'This is the real wonder drug of modern medicine, isn't it?' Callum said, taking a gulp of his coffee as he came back in. 'Maybe patients could get by without it, but doctors couldn't! Now, tell me about Bhasa Singh. You'll want to assess her breathing status before Friday's surgery with spirometry. . .'

'We ordered an X-ray this morning and that looked. . . well, as good as I'd hoped, but not better.'

They discussed it all in detail—the danger of slower-than-normal healing of the surgical site due to the steroids Bhasa was forced to take, a blood count and sediment rate to check for any signs of infection and the discontinuation of Bhasa's bronchodilator drugs—which might have elevated the heart rate to a risky level during surgery.

Then Callum drained the last of his coffee and reached for her empty cup as well, getting to his feet. 'I'm glad you'll be there, too, Megan,' he said matter-of-factly. 'She'll be drowsy from her pre-med but, all the same, if she gets scared of me again. . .'

'You handled that so well today,' she blurted out.

He shrugged, and that grin of his chopped across his face like a chunk of wood being axed out of a tree-trunk. 'It's happened before. Must be my thunderous eyebrows.' He moved his beetling brows up and down and she had to smile at his easy, comfortable capacity for self-mockery. 'Or my piratical expression.'

'All you have to do is smile, Callum, and anyone would—' She stopped abruptly. That was far too revealing an observation.

But he ignored her sudden silence. 'I don't expect it's a problem *you're* frequently faced with! You'd look like a fairy queen even if you scowled like a melodrama villain. Today especially in that soft pink.'

She flushed at his dispassionate assessment, and brushed pointlessly at the patterned pink and cream of the flowing skirt and matching blouse she wore beneath her white coat. There was no hint in his observation of personal flattery or a desire to compliment. He was simply speaking the truth as he saw it, and she felt again how meaningless her looks were. They created a first impression but, beyond that, others had to respect her—and she had to respect herself—on the inside.

Rising too, more anxious than ever to be out of the magnetic field he seemed to generate for her, she told Callum quickly, 'I'm sure it will go well, and it has to improve the long-term outlook for her respiratory problems. I'm looking forward to seeing you at work.'

'Don't do that!' He took her coffee-cup and she felt the brief, accidental touch of his fingers, triggering an electric pulse all through her as she entered the corridor. 'My theatre nurses all think I'm an ogre!' he flung after her.

It seemed highly unlikely.

Megan dreamed about ogres that night—female ogres, wearing silk scarves on their neat, greying hair. The next night she dreamed about pirates, threatening her with gory plastic models of the human heart, and both times, in the middle of the dream and at its most frightening point, Callum was suddenly there.

At first he was terrifying, too—a black, looming shape or a sudden suffocating form, imprisoning her—but then she realised that it was Callum and his form and his touch changed to become tender and safe then gradually passionate and heated—until she was tumbling in a headlong rush of sensation that was so real she awoke, tangled in her bedding and in tears because he wasn't really there.

On Friday morning, with last night's dream still refusing to relinquish its hold on her senses, she rose before six and went in to do early rounds as Bhasa Singh was first on Callum's list for the morning at eight o'clock.

Camberton Hospital's suite of operating theatres, which was just beginning to hum with activity, wasn't a place she needed to come to very often. In fact, she had to think hard about the last time she'd been present during surgery. Over a year ago, surely, with another chronically ill paediatric patient.

That was right. Julian Brown's lower bowel reconstruction. The little boy had been born with normal intelligence but a horrific list of congenital abnormalities, including the chest problems she'd dealt with for over a year, some of them requiring state-of-the-art surgery to correct. The surgeon on that occasion had been a visiting specialist from London. Now *he* really was an ogre, despite his internationally acknowledged brilliance. The operation had been successful that day, but you could have cut the tension in the room with an extra-blunt knife. . .

Theatre Sister Anne Dashwood found her a scrub suit in the usual dull green, then hurried off to Theatre One where an emergency orthopaedic procedure was just winding up. 'Mr Priestley's scheduled for Theatre Three today,' she called on her way out. 'He was in, but he's gone again. Go in there, if you like. They're setting up, and the patient is on her way. There are shoe-covers and masks and the rest of it along the wall there.'

Megan found what she needed and struggled a little with the shapeless shoe-covers. She was definitely rusty at this! Callum, though. . . It would be second nature to him. 'Theatre' was a fitting word to describe these elaborately equipped rooms. Callum was the star, and this was where he performed his virtuoso work. She couldn't help feeling the bite of curiosity. She knew so little about him, really, either as a surgeon or as a human being, her sense of the man so completely swamped by sensual memory and awareness. Maybe he *was* an ogre, or a boor. . .

Down the corridor she could see a wheeled stretcher being manoeuvred out of the lift and there was Bhasa, looking tiny against the white sheeting. She was very drowsy from her pre-med, but managed a watery, 'Hello, Dr Stoney-stone.'

Megan followed her into the theatre, after the nurses had formally identified Bhasa as the right patient in the right theatre for the right procedure, then Ron Rose quietly coached his registrar in readying her for general anaesthesia. There was another team here, too—those who would be responsible for setting up and maintaining a bypass of the heart and lung functions during the most critical part of the surgery.

Callum, as befitted his status, was last to arrive, accompanied by the dark young woman who was his registrar— Ariadne Demopoulos—training in this very demanding specialty herself. Against Callum's bulk she looked tiny, and lent a certain courtliness to his gesture of standing back while she was assisted into a gown.

'Hello, Bhasa,' he said gently to the little girl as he waited.

'Hello, Dr Calamine. . .'

'We're almost ready, OK. . .?'

But she was too drowsy to respond at all now, and in another minute Ron Rose would start her anaesthesia through the IV line which was already in place.

Callum now stepped over to be gowned, and Megan wasn't sorry. Surgical scrubs did nothing whatever to disguise his densely powerful figure. The cotton-polyester fabric, limp and faded from countless launderings, pulled across his back and thighs as he moved. . .and across his rear. Solid sinew, muscle and bone—every bit of him. Great handfuls of male flesh, blatant from head to toe. In another second he would turn around and she'd have to deal with a front view.

Megan turned away quickly herself and gabbled to Ron, 'She's so tiny.'

'Don't worry. I'm not giving her the professional rugby player's dose,' the balding anaesthetist grumbled through his mask. Megan caught the dry humour just in time, as Ron's registrar smirked dutifully in the background.

And Callum was ready.

Heart surgery was, perhaps, the ultimate in invasive procedures, Megan considered. Essentially she was an observer this morning, and could afford to philosophise internally over the incredible technology that allowed this group of trained professionals to actually reroute the body's blood supply so that it bypassed the heart and lungs and had those functions of pumping and oxygenation performed by machine.

'Looking good,' Ron murmured.

Callum's focus was intense now, communicated in the blaze of his green eyes above the mask, the lowering of his black brows beneath the cap, the practised movements of his fingers and the instructions he gave at intervals in a controlled, yet chatty tone to the scrub nurse, the bypass team and to the dark woman who was his registrar. 'Rectractor. . . No, the smaller one, please Ginny. . . Look, this is nice, isn't it? Holding nicely. . .'

With Bhasa's small body surrounded by drapes and instruments, machines and hands, Megan could see little of the actual procedure. She wasn't altogether sorry. At one point in her career, through sheer ambition, she had considered this very specialty. Heart surgeons had a god-like reputation—sometimes self-bestowed.

But she had neither the temperament nor the hands, as it turned out, and she'd found her niche far more comfortably in chest medicine, where there was more ongoing patient contact, more challenge to her skills in diagnosis, not quite as much life-and-death tension. . .and, to be honest, less blood!

Although this morning, with the heart function bypassed, the surgical field was remarkably clean and clear.

It was cold in the theatre. Hugging her arms around herself, Megan saw that Callum and his team were too busy to feel the chill but Ron looked across and rolled his eyes in sympathy. 'Getting there,' he murmured. 'She's doing fine. But, then, those asthmatic lungs of hers aren't involved at the moment.'

Some little time later Callum announced on an exhalation of breath, 'Right, that's as good as it's going to get. . .'

Megan looked across at Ron, alarmed, but he grinned and murmured, 'It's textbook perfect, Megan, don't worry. Callum always is.'

Relieved, she watched as the bypass team restored the heart and lung function, with co-operation from Callum and Ariadne, then wheeled their equipment away.

Why had she doubted Callum's competence, even for a moment? He exuded it from every pore, and the smooth give and take between the other members of the team told her that they had complete confidence in him too. She thought about Gary Henley and his inevitable need for a heart-lung transplant somewhere down the line. Such dramatic, cutting-edge surgery was not done here in Camberton, and Gary would probably go to Harefield Hospital in Middlesex for the operation once a donor for him was found.

But, with transplant surgery becoming more successful and more routine as techniques were refined and immuno-suppressant drugs perfected, perhaps Camberton Hospital would enter the field eventually. I'd love to give a patient like Gary to Callum, Megan thought. He would respond so well to that maleness in him, that warrior quality. We'd hear no talk of 'Dr Death' if Callum was involved. . .

But now was not the time to be speculating on Gary Henley's future, and a movement from Ron drew her attention back to him. He was intently focused at this point as Callum worked, the oesophageal stethoscope in his ears.

'OK, I'll lighten her a bit now. . .'

'Right, let's close,' Callum was saying. 'Ariadne?'

'Can I?'

'You *can*. And you *may*. Do you want to?'

'Yes, as long as you're—'

'I'm not going anywhere,' he growled, towering over her.

'Want to listen?' Ron said to Megan at the same time.

'Yes, please!'

'Sweet and clear as a bell,' the anaesthetist promised, as he passed the earpiece of the oesophageal stethoscope across to her.

Megan listened. With the other end of this special stethoscope actually sited in the oesophagus, directly beside the heart and between the two halves of the lungs, she could hear the heart and lung sounds with incredible clarity and, as Ron said, Bhasa's touchy respiration was nicely clear.

Then, all of a sudden, it wasn't. Ariadne had moved to take Callum's place and she must have stumbled. Reaching out to lever herself upright but wanting to protect her gloved hands, she landed an elbow heavily on tiny Bhasa's ribcage, jolting her dangerously. Ariadne gave a shriek, and there were sounds of dismay from everyone in the room.

Remembering the bowel reconstruction last year, and the London specialist's frequent and violent explosions of anger, Megan held her breath as Ariadne sputtered, 'Oh, my God! I'm sorry! Oh, my God, Callum!'

'Forget it,' he ordered, urgent but not threatening.

'I—'

'*Forget it! Now!*'

'I can't. . . I'm shaking. . .'

Then, through the stethoscope, Megan heard a sound more ominous than any surgeon's raised voice. 'She's gone into bronchospasm!' she rapped out. Ron grabbed the earpiece of the stethoscope roughly from her and stuffed it back in his ears.

'Bad!' he said. 'I'm turning off the nitrous oxide and putting her down deeper again.'

He did so, waited a little as everyone watched in tense silence and then said, 'No, she needs something more aggressive.'

He named a drug and there was a sharp reaction from Callum. 'That'll bump the heart up. I'm not sure it can take it at this stage. It could be very dangerous. If it pushes her into dysrhythmia. . .' He frowned blackly, then suggested, 'Steroids instead? Aminophylline?'

'No.' Megan shook her head. 'We already upped her steroids in preparation yesterday. It's too slow-acting to help now.'

'Aminophylline, sure,' Ron was saying, 'but I'm giving her the other stuff, too. Callum, I *have* to. I'll start with the minimum possible dose, but—'

'Get the bypass team back,' Callum ordered sharply. 'If it's too much for her heart. . .' He didn't finish, then turned to his registrar. 'Now, Ariadne, I want you to get ready to close as soon as we've got this stabilised.'

'No. No, I—'

'*I want you to finish this patient's surgery.*'

'No. . .'

Ron Rose met Callum's eye and muttered, 'I've got to increase it some more, Callum,' and Ariadne went white. Then at last, while Megan felt she still hadn't taken a proper breath since this sharp and unexpected crisis began, he added 'OK, she's responding. . .'

And the heart monitor, mercifully, still showed the

bumpy pattern of waves that they all recognised as normal. Ariadne continued to look rigid with horror.

'Ariadne,' Callum told her, gentle and iron-hard at the same time, 'you're standing here. You have to do it. I'm not letting you off the hook.'

He seized the first instrument she needed from the nurse at his side and thrust it into her hand then talked her through every tiny step for several minutes, somehow managing to split his focus between a knife-sharp attention to what she was doing and wordless eye-contact with Ron Rose. Was everything still as it should be?

At last Ariadne regained her control. 'I'm all right, Callum,' she said. 'I can do it now. Thanks. . .'

'Thanks, Callum,' Megan echoed some minutes later as she walked beside him down the corridor of the theatre suite. Her legs were still distinctly unsteady.

'For what?' He gave her a sliding, sidelong glance.

'For. . .saving her life?' she hazarded.

He gave a bark of laughter that crumpled up his rugged, compelling face. 'Rubbish! It was Ron did that.'

'Well, yes, but—'

'And the miraculous fact that her own heart didn't jump into dysrhythmia. I almost had her back on bypass without even waiting to see if she'd hold out.'

'And the fact that you'd just performed a very delicate and difficult surgical procedure in record time and with a total absence of fuss and trauma had nothing to do with her heart holding out, Callum?' She was absurdly eager to show him that her praise was sincere.

'All right.' He stopped abruptly in mid-corridor and gave an exaggerated bow, his tree-trunk of a torso bending with a fluid grace which might have surprised her if she hadn't had certain dark memories—*that night*—to call upon. 'I accept your thanks.'

He straightened and the fabric of his scrubs, which had

tautened as he bent, dropped loosely into place again. Despite the theatre's chill she saw that it was damp across his chest, drawing her focus to the broad patch of dark hair visible as a shadow beneath and curling thickly at the neck of the green tunic-style top.

'I—' Stop looking at him! 'You supported Ariadne, too.'

'What? Should I not? She's my registrar.'

'She picked a horrible time to lose her footing,' Megan pointed out. 'The last time I saw a surgeon in action he swore like a trooper at every member of the team, with far less cause. Even me!'

'Who was that?'

'Alan Blake.'

'Hmm.' He recognised the name. 'And what did you do to incur his wrath?'

'I'm still wondering. I was only observing, as I was today. Breathed at the wrong speed?'

He laughed, and she relaxed a little. Was this progress? A softening in their relations at last? He was standing back against the corridor wall now, one arm raised so that he could lean it at shoulder level on the scuffed paintwork. It was a very steady pose, physically distant—but, then, she wasn't asking for closeness, just a co-existence which didn't churn her insides every time they met.

'As for Ariadne,' he was saying, 'I'll have a good talk to her in private later. And she'll probably get a good tongue-lashing from me, at that! Alan Blake's right in one sense. A surgeon—anyone on the team, in fact—has to be able to take the pressure. I don't like increasing it by playing prima donna and I don't think humiliating a junior doctor in the middle of a surgical nightmare does anything for the patient—or anyone else—but the pressure's there, and if she can't deal with it. . .'

'I couldn't,' Megan admitted.

'No?' There was a flash of curiosity in his green gaze.

'No. I did think of it at one time, but I didn't have the right qualities.'

There was an odd silence and she was deeply aware of his scrutiny, taking in her face and slim figure—now clothed again in tailored black wool pants, modest heels and a silvery-grey silk blouse. His eyes might have been fingers—they seemed to awaken her nerve endings every bit as much as touch would have done.

'Probably to your credit,' he said finally. 'Good surgeons can be unbearable people.' He paused, and his strong face took on that fierce expression again as he added slowly, 'Too sure of themselves for their own good. . .or anyone else's.'

She stammered something meaningless, then he lifted himself off the wall and said briefly, 'I'll be out in a minute. You're going to find Mrs Singh?'

'Yes, to tell her—'

'Tell her I'll be out. It went well.'

Three strides later he had disappeared into the bathroom, the swing door gusting shut behind him, and Megan was alone, her legs—which had almost recovered at one point—now unsteadier than ever.

Too sure of themselves. Had he meant. . .? He *had* meant himself. Was it, after all this time, some gruff form of apology for his proud distance after that night? Surely not! She was the one who had behaved so badly.

'Thank God I didn't go into cardiothoracic surgery!' she muttered to herself as she hurried out of the theatre suite. 'He tortures me enough when I see him twice a week. If I had to see him every day. . .*in scrubs*. . .'

The sentence remained unfinished.

CHAPTER THREE

PLUNGED into her own work for the rest of the day, Megan didn't get a chance to see Bhasa again until her outpatient clinic had finished and she had dealt with sending off tests, returning phone calls and dictating notes into her small, hand-held recorder. In other words, after six o'clock. She hurried up to Paediatric Intensive Care, mentally calculating the time she could afford to spend there. She was going out tonight, and had to get home by a quarter to seven if she was to have a hope of being ready to leave again by seven-thirty.

It would be nice if she could look forward to the evening—gathering in a group for Derek Wyman's forty-ninth birthday dinner at a very smart restaurant, Partridge's, arranged earlier in the week by Gaye—but at the moment she felt far too tired.

Bhasa was asleep, watched over by her father, while Mrs Singh took a much-needed break at home. At this stage the little girl was still connected to a frightening array of tubes, drains and machines, and if medication kept her unaware of her condition for the next day or two that could only be for the best.

Megan talked quietly to Mr Singh for a few minutes, giving him her own perspective on the surgery, then looked at Bhasa's flow-sheets, alert to any potential problems. 'She's doing well,' was her assessment, and Mr Singh nodded.

'Mr Priestley says he's very pleased, too.'

'Oh, he was in recently?'

'He left only a few minutes ago.'

'Right, well, I expect I'll catch up with him soon,' she

answered, thinking to herself that it would probably be Monday at the earliest before she saw him. She planned to check on Bhasa tomorrow and no doubt he did too, but it was unlikely that their visits would coincide.

Having looked up in trepidation every time she heard movement outside the door of Bhasa's cubicle and steeling herself for the sight of Callum's disturbing bulk in the doorway, it was ridiculous to now feel *disappointed* that she had missed him. Once again she regretted the talk she'd had with Gaye. All it had done was to open an old wound and retard its healing.

Gaye. . . Time to leave. And it was good that she had missed Callum; good that she wouldn't see him until Monday. She could spend the weekend scolding herself into a more sensible perspective on the matter!

As it happened, though, Megan was denied this luxury of time. . .

Eager not to be late, she actually arrived at Partridge's early and only Gaye and Derek were there, having a drink in the comfortable bar as they'd arranged.

'You look *lovely*, Megan! Is the dress new?'

'No! Almost four years old!'

'But it's gorgeous. I've never seen you in it.'

'I forgot about it. Isn't that silly?'

She had worn it as one of six bridesmaids at a cousin's wedding, and hadn't liked it back then, thinking it too peasant-like and flowing at a time when she had favoured crisply sophisticated and tightly tailored clothing. Tonight, though, screeching the coat-hangers along the railing of her wardrobe—rejecting glittering black beading, a stiff silver sheath and a heavy moiré silk suit in bold pink—she had discovered it right at the back and found with surprise that she loved it on sight now.

Made of Paisley-patterned silk in colours of peacock blue, sea green and half a dozen more cool shades, it had a cropped cardigan jacket over a simple round neck and elbow-length sleeves and a skirt that flowed to her calves, soft and full, from a loose, gathered waist.

The violently spike-heeled shoes which matched the dress were a less welcome discovery but there was no other possibility in her shoe-rack and she put them on, wondering just why she had once thought it so important to have the extra poise and height at the expense of blistered heels, pinched toes and an aching lower back. . .

'Well, you just look fabulous!' Gaye was saying, her cheeks rather pink with excitement.

Excitement? Derek's birthday, presumably. Megan turned to the comfortably rotund older man with a quick kiss and her good wishes, and presented him with the frivolous packet of golf socks she had bought him. Gaye had said categorically, 'No presents! Derek's impossible to shop for!' but the Wymans had been so good to her over the past year or so. . .

'Don't open them now, Derek,' Megan ordered. 'They're too undignified for Partridge's.'

Gaye still looked excited. No, nervous, actually, and she was biting her bottom lip. She winced a little as she told Megan, 'I asked the McCarthys tonight, too, but they had a previous engagement, and the Hartmans dropped out at the last minute. Nina had to go to Leeds to oversee a critical operation, and their nanny had the flu so Richard is staying home with the children. I'm sorry, Megan. . .'

'Heavens, Gaye, that's all right. It's not your fault.'

'I know, but it means there'll only be. . .um. . .the four of us.'

'Four? Then who—?'

Gaye winced again, flashed her eyes towards the door and lifted a hand quickly in greeting before gazing at Megan once more with guilt, eagerness and mute apology a bizarre mix in her expression. 'I thought. . .' she gabbled. 'It was an impulse. If there'd been eight of us. . . But now it seems too *obvious*. Oh, dear!'

And, following her gaze across the room, Megan was very unsurprised to see Callum Priestley looming towards them. So much for not seeing him until Monday. He'd exchanged softly clinging and very faded scrubs for dark pants and a white shirt, but his dense body was as flagrantly apparent to Megan's gaze as if he'd been naked. She closed her eyes for a moment, struggling against the dangerous wash of her awareness, then opened them—to find him standing just feet away and mouthing gruff greetings as his focus flicked from Gaye to herself and back again.

Gaye still looked as guilty as a thief and her flustered words, falsely bright, betrayed far too much. 'Callum! I didn't tell you Megan was coming, did I? Or *did* I?'

'No, you didn't, Gaye,' he growled, shifting his weight from one leg to the other. 'Hello, Megan. Bhasa is doing well. Did you see her?'

'Yes, just after you'd left, apparently.' Megan seized on the subject gratefully. Callum knew as well as she did that this was matchmaking. She could see it in the proud wariness of his stance, the way his big shoulders were held so stiffly. But if they could collude in a wall-to-wall fog of medical talk, perhaps it could be papered over. 'Her pulmonary function—'

'No shop talk, you two!' Gaye came in brightly, and Callum's gaze met Megan's and clung for one desperate second. So much for that strategy! Would he think she had put Gaye up to this?

'Want a drink, Callum, Megan, before we go in?' Derek's hearty question brought heartfelt relief to everyone. If he was in on the plot he wasn't letting it show.

'Um. . .' Megan began and again her gaze collided with Callum's, to accurately read his shared reluctance. 'How about we sit down? I'll have wine with the meal, and I don't have. . .uh. . .a brilliant head for alcohol.' Indeed not! Three drinks and she became a siren, luring innocent

cardiothoracic surgeons into bed. Was Callum thinking of
it? Oh, he was. Of course he was, behind that careful
mask of a face. 'If that's all right with you, Derek,' she
finished feebly.

'Gaye and I have finished. We did have gin and tonic,
didn't we, at great extravagance? But I'm game for wine
as well.'

'Mmm, me too,' Gaye squeaked. As long as it didn't
loosen her matchmaker's tongue!

So they trooped in, with the two men leading—locked
in conversation—and Gaye pulled Megan back to whisper,
'I just thought. . . I've always thought that you two. . . And
if there'd been eight of us. . .'

'Please, Gaye,' Megan implored, 'don't do anything like
this ever again, will you? Callum doesn't—I don't—'

'As to that last thing, I don't believe you, madam! You
protest too much on the subject, but I know this *is* embarrassing. I won't do it again!'

Protest too much? Was Callum's effect on her that obvious? To *him*? Or only to Gaye? 'If you'd just let us talk
shop. . .' she begged.

'All right! All right!'

Ahead of her Callum's stride made the fabric of his
dark pants play against the dense forms of muscle beneath
and Megan felt the whispering silk around her own body,
tightening her pores—tightening her breasts into furled
buds at the tips. Did it show? Hastily she buttoned the
pretty jacket-top, then felt too stiff and formal and wondered if at some point she could dare to take it off. Surely
her body couldn't behave like this the whole evening?

Inevitably, over food, things settled down. Gaye forgot
her guilt and nerves, Callum rose to the occasion and
attacked Derek roundly on an issue of hospital policy and
he defended the administrative line with cheerful stub-
bornness.

Megan came to Callum's defence, although the prioritising of elective surgery wasn't an area that concerned her very often in the course of her own work, and she dealt with that flash of surprise. . .and something else. . .in the surgeon's green eyes at her support by staring down at her lobster bisque and taking several big, burning gulps of its rich flavour.

By the time they'd finished main courses of elegantly presented game fowl or steak, swimming in savoury sauces and accompanied by lightly steamed vegetables, Megan's white wine had gone to her head just enough for her to think happily, I'm safe! She surreptitiously levered her shoes off under the table and stretched her stockinged toes.

I'm not going to throw myself into his arms and beg him to make love to me behind the potted ferns, Gaye's not going to give off any embarrassing hints and dear Derek is so oblivious to the whole issue that he's keeping the conversation going beautifully—and I've managed not to look at Callum for at least half an hour.

Enjoying the bite of Callum's blunt wit and the froth of Gaye's interjections, she even went so far as to order dessert and coffee. Callum did, too, despite having already polished off the two most substantial dishes on the menu. Megan suspected he must eat like a horse to fuel that big body, which she knew—remembering with every nerve-ending—boasted not an ounce of superfluous fat.

Gaye and Derek shook their heads at dessert, though, patting their stomachs ruefully.

'Can't afford it,' Derek sighed.

'Claire's always throwing accusations of flab at us,' Gaye said. 'And I must say, when I look at my hips. . .'

But before the hazelnut torte and berry soufflé could arrive for Callum and Megan the waiter came to say, 'Mr and Mrs Wyman? There is a telephone call. . .'

'Not a hospital budget crisis at ten o'clock on a Friday night!' Gaye exclaimed.

'I believe it's your daughter. . .'

The Wymans exchanged glances. The two teenage girls
were alone at home. . .

'I'll go,' said Gaye, and when she came back to the
table five minutes later she was in a state of flustered
frustration. 'They've flooded the laundry. Heaven knows
how, but apparently a pipe's broken in some odd spot and
they can't get a bucket under it and it's just pouring out.
Claire actually called a plumber—she must be growing
up—but I don't like the idea of them being alone in the
house at night with some man we don't know. Derek,
we'll have to go straight away.'

She flung a pleading glance, reminiscent of earlier in
the evening, at Megan as Derek got to his feet. 'Coffee at
home, then, I suppose,' he said gloomily.

Gaye added, 'You two, though, don't worry. Enjoy your
dessert!' She put one arm around a shoulder of each of
them at the same time, which had the effect of drawing
them together as a couple. Megan tried to lean away again
without it being too obvious. 'This is just life in the dom-
estic war-zone, I'm afraid. I'm *so* sorry. . .' Her wince and
breathy apology left Megan in no doubt as to what she
meant—so sorry to leave you alone with Callum. And a
minute later the Wymans had gone, leaving Callum and
Megan and two regal-looking plates of torte and soufflé.

There was a lengthy silence and they stared at the food,
then Callum's seat creaked as he shifted. His effort was
visible. 'Yours looks good,' he said.

'Yes. So does yours.'

'Want to share?'

'Oh. . .' Before she could make a proper reply he'd
looked around the elegant restaurant, satisfied himself that
no one was watching and divided both torte and soufflé
into two precisely equal halves without a crumb or a drop
of berry juice out of place. He was a surgeon, after all.
He then whisked a piece of each onto each plate, whistled
softly under his breath, twiddled his thumbs and looked

at the ceiling, as if to say, It wasn't me, it was *her*!

Megan laughed.

'Can't take me anywhere, can you?' he said. 'Now, let's see, *was* it a fair exchange, or am I well punished for coveting your choice?' He tasted both of them and grinned. 'Well, I'm happy. . .'

Oh, God, what a relief! She'd have sat stiffly, bathed in awkwardness about this whole thing and certain that he would blame her for it, but he had come in so quickly with humour that there wasn't time for tension, and now they both began to relax. Somewhat. He was shifting in his seat again as he ate. In a hurry to get home? It was after ten now. . .

'Don't tell me! Do I get yours too?' he prompted after a minute, raising his strongly drawn eyebrows at her plate, and she realised that she'd forgotten to eat. Too busy *not* looking at him. . .

'Um. . . No, no, I—'

'Ah! You're in collusion with the unions, are you? If you stall long enough the kitchen staff will move into overtime rates.'

'Yes, that's it,' she managed lamely.

Silence again. There were just the two of them at the table, and the restaurant was emptying now. She could see only two other couples—no, not 'other' couples; she and Callum weren't a couple—at distant tables. The lighting seemed lower than it had been earlier, as if the waiters had decided that an atmosphere was needed.

She heard Callum clear his throat, and forked in another light mouthful of soufflé. Get this finished. Get home, away from him, while she still had her dignity intact. Cross Gaye off her Christmas card list as soon as she got home and *never* speak to the meddling woman again!

And just what was Callum's hand doing, reaching across the table to touch her cheek? 'Berry juice,' he said. 'Gone now.'

Heart thudding, Megan nodded breathlessly. His touch stayed like a streak of paint on her face.

With their plates empty at last, both of them gulped their coffee. Their gazes kept meeting, clashing, locking, tearing apart. He was flushed now, and she knew that she had been flushed the whole evening. The salty, hearty effect of his humour had gone. She hadn't met him halfway because she'd racked her brains and couldn't think of a thing to say. He must be disgusted with her. He looked it, and wasn't making an effort any more.

He summoned the waiter with one lift of his big hand— that white shirt rippled across his shoulder again—and then thrust it into his jacket pocket, questing for his wallet.

'The bill has been settled already, sir.'

'Right.' He shifted, threw a look at Megan and she recognised her cue with a perverse and quite ridiculous disappointment. . .then remembered that her shoes were still beneath the table.

Fumbling discreetly with a foot, she located one and slipped it on without incident but the second shoe seemed to have disappeared. Her bare foot was waving about wildly now and she didn't realise that the rigid object she kept encountering with her calf was Callum's leg until she suddenly caught sight of his face, tight with embarrassment. He looked like a hunted, suffering creature.

Oh, God, he thinks I'm playing footsy!

She blurted, 'My shoe. I kicked it off and I've lost it.'

The tortured look evaporated and he muttered, 'That's what it is, then, that I've been treading on all evening,' before twisting to reach beneath his chair. How on earth had it migrated that far?

Straightening, he pushed himself back a little and ordered, 'Stick out your foot!'

'Wh—?'

'Discretion, Dr Stone!' he pleaded. 'I'll slip it on, then we don't have to go passing it across the top of the table.'

'Right. . .' Reluctantly, she gave him her foot beneath the white swathe of the tablecloth and felt the warmth of his big hand enclosing it gently. He looked at her across the table as he tried to match foot and shoe, and that tortured look was back on his face. His fingers tickled and thrilled and he evidently didn't understand too much about women's shoes because it wasn't going on easily.

'Well, you're certainly no Cinderella,' he muttered drily, then at last her foot slipped in, they both—in unconscious unison—gave breathy sighs of relief and she felt again those paint-streaks of sensation as his fingers trailed across her ankle and he let her go.

Walking just in front of him from their table, she heard the brush of his trousers as his thighs met in mid-stride and felt the heat of him so close to her own bare forearms. She had taken off the silk jacket earlier and didn't bother to put it back on now. Then, suddenly, she was confronted by the big mirror in the entrance-way, and by her reflection and Callum's just behind her. It was a startling, perfect picture for an instant: his dark, dense bulk towering behind her; her own fair beauty and softly pretty clothing, her slenderness emphasised by his strength.

They were a study in contrasts—dark and light, heavy and fine, solid and flowing—and she thought, with desire clamouring in her and making her almost ill, This is how it should be. This is the way a man and woman should join—when they're so outwardly, physically different, like the chemical reaction between two compounds. Is that why *that night* was so explosive?

He had frozen for a minute too, watching the picture they made. Their eyes met in the mirror, and it was all she could do not to sink back against him.

She watched as he collected her black suede coat and held it out for her, seeing his movement in the mirror and wondering if they would happen to touch. She wanted it so badly that she trembled with the effort of keeping herself

contained, and when he—stiffly, very deliberately—
managed to heap the coat onto her shoulders without
touching her, her disappointment was so intense that her
breath gusted from her lips in a movement too violent to
be called a sigh.

He was furious. She could see how set his face was,
and she thought miserably, He's been putting on an act
all evening. He's hated this, every minute of it, and he
only behaved so wonderfully, making me laugh, because
he knew it was easier that way.

They walked in silence to their cars, keeping further
apart now that they were in the open. He had a utility van
these days, not the vehicle he'd driven two years ago—
that night. It was an unusual choice for a doctor and
she wondered about it. Wondered, that is, until she was
distracted by his wooden question a few seconds later, 'Is
that your car?'

'Yes.' It was red and sporty-looking, but fairly ordinary.

'You've got a flat tyre.'

'Hell!'

'I'll help change it.'

'No, no. . .' His reluctance was palpable, and she'd
rather risk ruining this dress than be in his debt. Then she
said, 'I can't change it.'

'I've just said—'

'I left the spare at the garage and forgot to pick it up.'

'Forgot? When was this?'

'Um, April? I'll just have to leave the car here until
tomorrow.'

He groaned through gritted teeth, but suppressed it
quickly. 'I'll give you a lift, then.'

'No. . .'

'Get in, Megan.' With heavy patience.

He unlocked the passenger door and she did then
directed him to her place, speaking at intervals between

which they drove in a silence which neither even tried to break.

I'm tired, Megan thought. It's Friday. And, anyway, this is nothing new. Callum and I have been like this for two years.

He pulled up outside her ultra-modern block of flats and didn't switch off the engine. Didn't even put on the hand-brake. She could see the red reflection of his rear brake-lights in the glass doors of the foyer, going on and off as he squeezed his foot impatiently up and down on the brake pedal.

'Callum, I'm sorry about the tyre. It...it was stupid and very female of me to forget.'

'Don't worry about it,' he answered—wary, careful— and then, in the same tone, 'This...wasn't your idea, was it?'

'The *tyre*?'

'The evening.'

'No.'

There was the tiniest pause, then he said, 'No, I didn't think so. Well, tell Gaye...not to do it again, thanks.'

'I already did... Callum, can't we just...forget about what happened two years ago?'

'Yes. Sure. Of course we can. I hoped you...we had,' he replied abruptly.

'It was all—I don't want—'

'Please!' he cut in. 'You said forget it. I respect that. In fact...I agree. Any sort of apology after all this time would be—'

'Would it? Yes. Yes, I expect you're right,' she conceded lamely.

'So let's just do it, forget it, and not say things we'll regret. OK?' A steel mask of an expression shuttered his features, and he shifted roughly. Why did he keep doing that? It made her so conscious of his powerful maleness every time those shoulders of his moved in the confines

of his shirt. She wanted to lay her head there as she had
once done, and feel the slow-burning fire of his passion
mounting and mounting. . .

'OK,' she managed. 'OK, Callum. . .'

She stumbled out of the car, and by the time she reached
the safety of the lighted foyer he was driving away.

By late the next morning she knew she had to talk to him
again. She had dealt with the problem of her car first thing
so that was one niggling issue out of the way, but then
in Intensive Care—visiting Bhasa after seeing two other
patients on the chest ward briefly—she was so churned
up at the slight possibility of seeing Callum that her head
was pounding and her stomach threatened to reject its
breakfast.

Bhasa was awake now, though still heavily medicated,
and she was fretful and needed distraction from the discomfort of the tubes and monitors still attached to her.
Oddly neither of the little girl's parents were there, and
she was fretting about this, too.

Megan stayed for quite a while and even read her a
story, which she didn't think Bhasa really listened to but
perhaps the tone was soothing. She certainly found it
soothing herself and thought, with a degree of resignation
because it was starting to seem fairly unlikely that it would
ever happen, Maybe I'd be good at this—this mother stuff.

She kept expecting the Singhs to appear. Or Callum.
He had to let her apologise more fully. Surely he could
give her that? *Surely* he could? And finally the tension in
her grew so unbearable that she asked the ICU ward sister,
who was busy at the nurses' station, 'Where are the
Singhs?'

'Oh, no one told you?'

'No. . .'

'Mrs Singh went into labour this morning. While Mr
Priestley was here, actually. He rang Mr Singh and

took her across to Maternity, but we haven't heard anything yet.'

'Does Bhasa know? She's worried. . .'

'Mrs Singh didn't want her to know. Mr Priestley came back and told her that her mother was resting. . .' so she'd missed Callum twice '. . .but I think she suspects something is up.'

'I'll stay a bit longer, then.'

So she did, holding Bhasa's warm relaxed little hand until the child slipped into a doze, her thoughts churning back and forth like a load of laundry in a noisy machine. Did he really think I would have engineered that evening? He must still have a terrible opinion of me! I suppose, judging by my past performance. . . I must let him know he needn't fear any awkward scenes. This has gone on too long. Surely we can start again on some footing that's easier for both of us!

Leaving the hospital at eleven, she gritted her teeth and decided, I'll go to his flat now, on the way home. I won't phone first. I'd only stammer and mess it up.

She remembered only too well where he lived. It had been like a sore spot on the face of the small city for two years. She was aware of the place every time she drove near it, had had to reject several impulses to drive down the street and knew immediately today, when she arrived, which letter-box and which flight of stairs were his.

But she had to stand outside his bland, closed door for a good ten minutes, rehearsing her words, before she summoned the courage to ring the bell. 'Callum, I think we need to talk honestly about—' 'Callum, I need you to forgive me, *really* forgive me for what happened!' 'Callum, you were wrong last night! You do have to give me the chance to apologise. Don't cut me off! There's too much unfinished business between us!'

At last she lifted her hand, its palms damp, and heard the peal inside the flat.

'Yes?'

Open-mouthed and with her stomach churning again, Megan faced the sharp-featured but exceedingly attractive redhead who had appeared and voiced the impatient question. The woman continued, 'Look, we're not interested in door-to-door charity or sales.'

A male voice, singing tuneless snatches of song along with the radio, filtered over the redhead's shoulder. Callum. . .

'I'm not—' Megan stopped. 'Sorry, I must have the wrong—'

She fled.

Callum lived with someone. Or did she have the wrong flat? She *didn't*! He lived with someone. No wonder his manners had slipped a few times last night. Why hadn't he told Gaye he wanted to bring his girlfriend? He was a very private man in so many ways. Perhaps the relationship was a new one and he wasn't yet ready to have gossip spread on the subject over the whole hospital. The redhead wasn't from the hospital. Megan was fairly sure about that.

I've lost him. I've really lost him now.

But, come, now, had she really thought there was a chance that her demand for a talk might lead to a rekindling of that brief, disastrous flame that so haunted her? Yes, oh, yes, silly Megan, admit it! Have you actually decided that this is the man for you, you fool? Talk about not learning from your mistakes!

Miserably she drove home and spent the rest of the weekend making a total mess of the angora sweater she was knitting for herself, until rescued on Sunday evening by an invitation from Rob Baxter to supper and a movie. He kissed her at the end of it in the car outside her flat, with rain streaming down the windows, and they were both forced to acknowledge the entire absence of chemistry between them.

'Tell me the truth, am I a profoundly unsexy man?'

he wanted to know, his tone a provocative drawl.

'I think it's me, Rob,' she told him humbly. Then, with reluctant honesty, she added, 'I'm hung up on a man who—'

'Doesn't know you exist?'

'Knows I exist. Wishes I didn't!'

'Ouch!' A grimace pleated his fair, smooth face, and he added lightly, 'A professional opinion from you, then, since we're trading confessions. . .'

'Yes? For what it's worth. . .'

'Ariadne Demopoulos. Could she possibly look with favour upon a humble cardiologist?'

'After the near-disaster she created in Bhasa Singh's surgery on Friday. . .'

'Ah, yes. . . Heard about that from Ron Rose.'

'. . .I'd say she'd probably like to *be* a humble cardiologist. Anything that doesn't involve wielding a scalpel!'

'Seriously, though. . .'

'Seriously, though, she's fairly new here and I haven't heard rumours that she's attached. I have the impression that she's nice, and she's certainly nice-*looking*. Why don't you try?'

'I think I will. . .'

So they ended the evening with prospects in the wind for one of them, at least. Megan, meanwhile, was deciding that she had better find something more meaningful and active to do with her spare time than knitting, raising money for an MRI scanner and seeing movies with men she only fancied very mildly and from the eyebrows upwards.

CHAPTER FOUR

'DR STONE?'

'Yes, Bhasa?'

'I love Dr Calamine!'

'Do you, love?'

'Yes, he's so *silly*!' Bhasa snuggled up to Callum's arm, which appeared nearly as thick as the child's fine-boned torso and far more powerful. He stretched to accommodate the gesture, having to hold himself rather clumsily to avoid toppling onto the bed where Bhasa lay.

It was Tuesday morning. Bhasa was out of Intensive Care now but her incision was still a raw line down the middle of her chest, and she was still being very carefully monitored.

'Could you let go now, Bhasa?' Callum pleaded, and when she did he ruffled her hair. 'You're just a little monkey, aren't you? You'd use me for a jungle-jim if I let you!'

'I'm not a monkey. But you're a great big gorilla. Only you're not fierce. Can I see the pictures of your pets?'

Bhasa longed for pets of her own but wasn't allowed to have them because of her asthma, and was wistfully fascinated by anyone else's—even the humblest hamster. Megan wondered about Callum's pets. Two dogs? Almost as big as he was?

'Let Dr Stone have a look at you first,' he answered.

'Oh, no, I can wait,' she blurted out, absurdly eager to be on a good footing with him. 'And. . .and I'd like to see your pets, too.' Which was pretty idiotic.

He raised his eyebrows at her—she couldn't blame him—and got out the pictures. As he did so, Bhasa said chirpily, 'I've got a new baby brother that I'll show *you* a picture of! He came on Saturday and Mam's pretty busy now. She's dying for me to see him. Probably tomorrow. So Dad's coming instead to sit with me. Soon!'

It was still early, and both Megan and Callum were making an informal visit to Bhasa before a longer and more official round later in the morning. Callum had got here first and Megan would have sneaked out and come back later, except that they had both seen her in the doorway. Now, having accepted the painful pleasure of seeing him, she didn't want to leave. Callum passed several photos over to Bhasa and said, 'Choose one to keep, if you like.'

'Yes, please! I'm not allowed to have pets because they make me wheeze.'

Standing on the opposite side of the bed from Callum, Megan could see the pictures quite clearly. There were canaries, which surprised her, and it suddenly struck her that the background to the bright birds in their cage showed a diamond-paned window with pink climbing roses and out-of-focus shrubbery beyond. It was absolutely *not* the view from the flat where she had spent *that night* two years ago.

'Have you moved, Callum?' she said suddenly, and saw his surprised glance once more.

'Yes, last year.'

'Oh.' So much for the redhead. Not that it was important.

Megan looked at Bhasa's chart, listened to her chest, asked some questions and satisfied herself that the various drugs she had prescribed seemed to be doing their job very well at the moment. The nursing staff had reported nothing untoward, and Callum was obviously pleased as well.

Guessing that he was almost ready to leave Bhasa's bedside too, she said a quick goodbye to the little girl and hurried—not to say scuttled—away, only to realise with a sinking heart when she reached her office and looked at the pathology reports that had come in since the weekend that she had two more patients to refer to him for surgery. Both men were smokers, and both had suspected bronchial carcinoma.

One of them, she felt, was a candidate for rigid bronchoscopy and the other, who was more seriously ill, needed a complete lung biopsy. They were not the kind of problems which could be quickly despatched by one phone call.

Reluctantly she picked up the phone and reached his secretary and they played duelling appointment diaries for several minutes, with Cecily Stark being surly, extremely stubborn and over-protective of Callum's time. His lunch hours were sacrosanct, and that half-hour before the lecture he was giving late this afternoon gave him an inviolable period in which to peruse his notes.

I do wonder why she dislikes me so much! Megan thought wearily.

They finally settled on five o'clock the following afternoon. 'And if that's not convenient for him after all there'll be a memo on your desk after lunch with an alternative time,' Mrs Stark decreed.

Megan rang off, resisting the temptation to suggest that the whole discussion be conducted by memo and that, in fact, since Callum's time was so hallowed why didn't he just perform all his surgery by memo as well? Was his secretary acting on the boss's orders in being so cold and unhelpful? No, that wasn't Callum's style, surely!

She had a long day, shuttling all over the hospital, including two calls down to Casualty. Wednesday was a repeat performance, so that when Callum came down to her office at five—there had, after all, been no memo on her desk after lunch the day before—she was still shuffling the sheafs of notes on her desk and trying to collect her thoughts.

Mr Swinnard's lung cancer had been caught early, if the tests performed so far were accurate, and she hoped that it would be possible for Callum to isolate the carcinoma by bronchoscopy and remove only a small portion of the lung the following week to leave fifty-six-year-old Martin Swinnard in good health.

Alfred Turnbull had ignored his symptoms for a long time and, sadly, his prognosis was not good. Megan expected that a surgical biopsy would reveal diffuse small-cell carcinoma, which carried a very poor prognosis for survival beyond a few months. She wasn't even sure that putting him through the discomfort of the biopsy was worthwhile, and had considered calling in a specialist oncologist for his opinion as well as Callum's.

She stumbled through the patient histories, distracted by his big body flung untidily into the chair across from her desk, and thought to herself, I was handling it better than this a few weeks ago. What's changed? I should *never* have said anything to Gaye!

'I'll add Mr Swinnard to my list on Monday,' Callum said, after he'd been given the full picture, including X-rays, test results and patient history. 'There's no sense in wasting time. Has he stopped smoking?'

'Well, his wife told him she'd divorce him straight away if he didn't,' Megan said.

'Ah, stuck between the devil and the deep blue sea!' A grin broke out on his face. 'The key question, then, is, is he happily married? Is divorce a dire threat or a rosy promise?'

'He's stopped smoking, Callum,' she told him drily, and he had the grace to look chastened. She added, with a touch of tartness in the humour, 'I take it you have little faith in marriage as an institution?'

But he didn't toss off some chauvinistic comment as

she'd half-expected, and his uncompromising face was serious as he said, 'I think the institution is bloody amazing. But it's like a lot of things, perhaps—greater than the sum of its parts. It can be the best blessing in the world for two people who manage to make it work, and a curse for those who don't.'

'Yes, that's true.' She suppressed a shiver, thinking of her own parents and the black farce they were still enacting together.

'You look as if you know what I'm talking about.'

'Mmm,' she nodded, unwilling to go into details. Their eyes met, and she didn't need him to tell her—he'd had an unhappy childhood, too.

But, my God, *how* had they got into this in the space of a few minutes? Deliberately she brought the focus back to their other patient, Alfred Turnbull, and Callum said, 'Doesn't look good, does it?'

'No, but he's at least trying. He's stopped smoking and drinking completely—and, yes, his daughter confirms that—and he's gone on some anti-cancer diet which sounds balanced and nutritious even if it can't possibly deliver what he wants it to.' She spread out her hands. 'The biopsy will give him a time-frame to adjust to, if nothing else, and we'll have a clearer picture for the palliative care people. And perhaps we're wrong, and radical surgery might—'

'With small-cell carcinoma? Removal of a complete lung? At his age?'

'I know. I could have cried when he told me how long he'd been postponing that crucial visit to his GP.'

There was a silence. Nothing else to say. Callum got quickly to his feet, the chair creaking from the release of his dense bulk. He had said no to coffee earlier, so there was nothing to keep him here and, from that faintly hunted look—that careful neutrality in his features—Megan could see that he was going to tactfully avoid staying a second longer than he had to.

All right, Callum. . .

Then suddenly it *wasn't* all right, and the part of her that had always believed in the power of her own will— had *had* to believe in it or she would have been emotionally destroyed as a child—took hold and blurted out to his departing back, 'Look, couldn't we go for. . .for a drink?'

He turned slowly, studying her from beneath his black brows. God, he was a forbiddingly virile man, and her heart turned over like a pancake flipping every time she laid eyes on him! She wanted to cradle that fiercely compelling face between her hands and read every detail of it with her lips.

'Yes, if you like,' he said at last. 'The Lion of Aragon?'

'Yes. I—I was going to suggest that.' Not like last time, when being surrounded by strangers had thrust them so dangerously into intimacy. 'That way—'

'We don't have to take our cars,' he finished for her. 'You've got your spare tyre back?'

'Yes,' she informed him humbly, heroically resisting the desire to make an abject apology for that little occurrence. 'And the other one fixed, too.'

'Good! Don't let yourself get in the same predicament again!'

To her relief, his eyes were twinkling and she managed a light, 'Yes, so very female, wasn't it? Almost as bad as not being able to change a light bulb which I do regularly, honestly I do! The feminist in me was deeply mortified at being caught out with no spare.'

'Promise I won't tell anyone.'

'Good, and I'll happily pay you a monthly stipend for your silence.'

'Ah, that'll come in handy, that will. You can keep me in Cuban cigars. . .or maybe vintage port.'

'Now, which will ruin your health faster?'

'Evil creature!'

They both laughed, their eyes met and suddenly the awkwardness was back after the easy banter. If she could have thought of anything else extremely silly to say, she would have. Of course, too much effort was the death of humour and nothing would come.

So she gathered her coat and bag and, instead, they both busily filled the space between them on the walk from the hospital to the pub with pointless chatter about car trouble and garage mechanics and petrol prices until, when he'd steered her firmly to the very prominent bar stools right by the till, she couldn't stand it any longer and said to him, in a low and fierce voice, 'It's no good! Callum, you *do* have to let me apologise for what happened two years ago.'

'Let *you* apologise?'

'Yes! You said the other night you thought it was too late for that, but that's unfair. You're denying me the opportunity to tell you I know how badly I behaved that night; to. . .to explain it if I can and make you—'

'How badly *you* behaved?' His voice was positively hoarse with disbelief and indignation as he struggled against sheer speechlessness to cut in.

'Yes!' she hissed. Why the hell did he have to make this so hard?

'My God, Megan, *I* was the one who behaved badly. Your coldness and distance afterwards told me how angry you were and I don't blame you for that in the least. I've wanted to apologise for two years, only—'

'Callum, you can't seriously be—'

'—I thought it'd just make things worse.'

They were leaning towards each other, both scowling, their voices raised above the noise of the pub to the level of hoarse, fiercely angry whispers.

'For heaven's sake, no!' she hissed at him. '*I* was the one who was falling all over you—'

But he was scarcely listening. 'I was afraid an apology would seem too shallow—'

'—And I think I knew it even as it happened, which is what makes it so terrible.' Their heated phrases duelled with each other.

'But, believe me, I know perfectly well that what I did was wrong. I took advantage of you. . .'

'I virtually seduced you.'

'Let's face it, I seduced you.'

Those last two phrases came in perfect unison. There was a sudden halt in their angry, overwrought tirade, and a sizzling awareness grew in the air between them. Callum was the first to speak. 'Oh, come on! Do you think that you could have got me to take you home if I hadn't wanted to? I was the one in control. I was the one who should have taken resp—'

'Oh, so now it's a competition, is it?' she accused wildly. 'An issue of power and control, and you want to win.'

'Not at all. But if you think I'm going to sit here and let *you* take the blame for what was evidently a night you must have loathed to the very marrow of your—'

'Loathed? My God, *loathed*, Callum Priestley?' she muttered. 'It was the best night of my life.'

'It was?' he rumbled fiercely then stopped, realising what she'd said. 'It *was*? Well. Good. Mine too, if you want to know.'

'But I was the one who—'

'Megan, *I* was the one who—'

'Surgical post-mortem, anyone?' said Rob Baxter, coming up and putting a heavy arm around each of them. Then he back-pedalled a little. 'Or is that already what this is about?'

'Er, no, it's not, actually,' Callum growled.

'Well, you were certainly going at each other,' the cardiologist accused cheerfully. 'I could see you from the door. Couldn't *hear* unfortunately. God, I'm tired!'

They both wished heartily that he would go away.
Megan could see her own sinking reluctance mirrored in
Callum's uncompromising face, but at the moment Rob
was blind to that sort of perception. His eyes were blood-
shot. He must have had a heavy on-call last night, and it
was quite obvious that he wasn't going to go away until
he'd had a beer and talked off the adrenalin that was
keeping him going.

Callum gave a tiny shrug of acceptance and shared the
ghost of a guilty smile with Megan, and then suddenly
they were both struggling against laughter. Verbally brow-
beating each other over the right to take the blame?
Competing viciously in their determination to win the right
to claim to have been wrong? It was absurd. . .and it meant
that they'd been badly at cross-purposes for two years.

For one brief moment she wondered, Does this
mean. . .? Could we pick up where we. . .?

Remembered sensation flooded her. Him and her. Man
and woman. So dark and so fair. In his bed. Tangled.
Joined.

No. . . No! Be realistic! Too much time had passed.
Beyond everything, it was destined to remain a one-night
stand. He couldn't possibly still want her, the way she—

'Megan? Focus!' The barman had appeared at last, and
Rob was pressing for her order.

'Oh, I can't. . .' she waved her hands vaguely. 'Whatever. Beer. What you're having.'

Callum wanted beer as well and, under the cover of
Rob giving the order, the two of them exchanged wary,
tentative smiles.

'Talk about misleading symptoms! Are we idiots?' he
wanted to know.

'I think so.'

'Then, how about if we agree to accept each other's
abject, grovelling apologies and leave it at that?'

'It. . .it sounds like the. . .er. . .most sensible—'

'Mature?'

'Mature plan, yes.'

'Alternatively, we could duel to the death over it, which would be—'

'Perhaps unnecessarily dramatic.'

'Indeed. I think we've reached consensus.'

'Oh. . . Good.'

Beyond their words there were things not being said, but Megan didn't quite know or trust what they were.

Their beers were slung across the bar. Rob took three gulps of his, rumpled his fair hair and pressed fingers into his bleary eyes. Clearly they were going to have to follow his conversational lead. It was probably for the best. He said to Callum, 'So. . .how's the elephant house?'

'That's finished,' the latter growled with some unwillingness. 'Cosy as a country cottage. It's the other place that's giving me trouble.'

'Bitten off more than you can chew?'

'Of course,' the surgeon grinned. 'Which I knew when I took it on. I like a challenge! But the place spooks me a bit with winter coming on, working there alone once it's dark outside.'

'Haunted, is it?'

'By the products of my imagination. Some of the people who once lived there can't have been all that happy. I think of it, and it gets to me.'

'Get some helpers in,' Rob suggested, yawning. 'People would, don't you think?'

'Would *you*?'

'No,' he admitted easily, 'but I'm selfish. I like watching football in my free time. And you wouldn't want to find out what I *can't* do with hammers and paint!'

Elephant house? Megan, in between the two men, was following this conversation in blank silence, and Rob suddenly realised the fact. He seemed incredulous. 'You haven't heard of this bloke's millstone of a project?'

'No. . .' I've steered well clear of hearing anything at all about Callum Priestley for two years.

'He's bought this great Victorian pile that has ''compassionate euthanasia'' written all over it. . . Really, Callum, you typical sawbones of a surgeon, trying to keep a suffering piece of architecture alive with your heroic intervention when it would be far better off if a big bull-dozer just put it out of its misery. . . And he's doing it up as a charitable institution.'

'Somebody had to,' Callum said gruffly.

'Nobody would have. The place would have been pulled down.'

'Which is why somebody had to do something.'

'It's hideous!'

'It won't be when I've finished with it.'

'Callum, it's innately, structurally hideous, down to the very marrow of its stucco-covered bones! It looks like a collision between mad King Ludwig's castle and a circus train pulled by Thomas the Tank Engine.'

'Well, that's basically what it is, Rob,' he said patiently, quite unperturbed.

'It sounds fascinating,' Megan cut in, intrigued by Rob's blunt and colourful description. It must be what he'd meant by 'elephant house'. As in 'white elephant'? Hideous, though? She wondered. . . She suspected these days that the gap between ugliness and beauty wasn't nearly as wide as most people thought and that the two qualities could come full circle and meet, as they did in Callum Priestley's fiercely virile face. . .

'It *is* fascinating,' Rob acknowledged. 'Callum deserves everyone's applause for taking it on.'

'Why did you, Callum?' The beer had already embold-ened her. Not the way the wine had done two years ago— thank goodness. She wasn't going to let herself off the hook. . .and she certainly wasn't going to make the same mistake twice! But she was suddenly aware of how very much more to Callum Priestley there was than just his uncompromising physique and her own demonic memories of the night they'd spent together.

'I thought it should be done,' he answered, turning to her, his big shoulder not touching hers but close. 'I just happened to drive past the place one day about two and a half years ago. It's on an alternative route between my old flat and the hospital. And I saw it was for sale. I thought straight away what a good position it had, and what potential. It was open that weekend so I took a look round—along with half a dozen other people who had no intention whatever of buying it—then got on the phone to several charities and institutions the following Monday, thinking they'd jump at it.'

'And didn't they?'

'They all knew of it already. The executor of the estate had approached them. But one lot had no capital; another lot couldn't get a committee formed to debate the issue. Someone-or-other's Children's Trust thought the place needed too much work. It did, too. Still does. For years it was illegally subdivided into a rabbit warren of little bedsits.

'And Camberton Hospital itself had just bought another smaller place—Hallam House, you know, where they're doing diabetic education and various counselling groups now—so they didn't want it. About four groups did but they just couldn't get themselves organised; couldn't take the risk of not getting council approval, and so on, and so on.

'Well, it didn't sell and it didn't sell and the price kept coming down, and the months passed and the weeds in the grounds got higher. I said to myself that if it dropped another two thousand pounds I'd bloody well buy it myself!'

'And it did?' Megan suggested.

He nodded. 'It did.'

'Put up a notice at the hospital,' Rob said, restive. He must have heard all this before. 'Have a few working bees. Offer food and beer at the end of the day.'

'It's a thought,' Callum said slowly. 'But, no. I don't want a whole crew of people who've come mainly for the social possibilities.' Then that white grin of his broke onto his face and he hummed a snatch of song, with exaggerated drama—'The Impossible Dream,' from *Man of La Mancha*. He had a more than adequate singing voice, Megan realised. 'I'm arrogant, I suppose,' he went on. 'Like the idea that I could do it myself. Oh, I wouldn't mind a couple of people who were really interested. . .'

'And who'd let you take all the credit,' Rob teased. 'A monument to your vision.'

'That's right. The Callum Priestley Home for Incurable DIY-ers.'

'I am,' Megan said suddenly, surprising all three of them. 'Interested in helping, that is.' She flushed. 'And it sounds as if you *deserve* all the credit, Callum.'

'Yes,' he agreed on a sigh. 'It was a crazy thing to do, and all my own fault. . .'

'Talking of crazy. . .' Rob launched into an anecdote about his partner in crime, Consultant Cardiologist Lloyd Sadler, and they didn't get back to the subject of Callum's white elephant. Rob was fading fast. He admitted it several minutes later. 'I got two hours of sleep. I'm crashing now.'

'Get home before it hits,' Callum advised. All three of them knew the feeling, though it was never as intense these days as it had been during those first couple of years after medical training when house officers were under the—sometimes justified—impression that they ran the entire hospital.

'I'd better,' Rob said, pouring the last of his beer down his smooth throat.

There was silence after he'd gone, and Megan wished

that she'd made her own departure on the tail of his. It was too late now. She had better sit for a little longer. Her intense exchange with Callum earlier had been interrupted in full swing, but somehow she didn't want to try and recapture the flow. There could be considerable danger in any more honesty. If Callum suspected that she'd still fall into his arms at the drop of a wine glass she'd be back to square one.

He said suddenly, 'Are you serious about wanting to help?'

For a moment she didn't even understand what he meant, then said, 'Your house?' He had said nothing earlier when she had made the unexpected offer, and she had assumed, sensibly unsurprised, that he didn't want her. Now what should she say? 'Y-yes, I'm. . .looking for something a bit different to do.'

'Well, this is different, all right,' he growled.

'And I won't last more than half an hour?' She recognised his unstated scepticism.

'Let's say three hours, and we'll call it a bet. If you're still there I'll make you dinner.'

'You're on!'

'Saturday afternoon? Two o'clock?'

'Two o'clock it is.'

It was a day of watery sunshine and chilly winds, and Callum had warned her that the heroic old Aga in the kitchen of his house couldn't raise the temperature very much. After toying with the idea of dressing to kill in some cute little parody of a workman's outfit, she'd taken him seriously and put on thickly fleeced grey jogging pants and an old navy cable-knit pullover, woollen ski socks and grubby leather running shoes—and felt delightfully comfortable and embarrassingly grungy.

After a busier-than-usual end to the work week, during which she and Callum had seen quite a bit of each other while dealing with her two new cancer patients, it was good to be out of the hospital.

She followed the directions he had given her without difficulty and he was waiting for her on the crumbling cement of the front steps, wearing age-softened and paint-stained jeans which moulded themselves to his strong legs and a black sweater with frayed sleeves. His canvas shoes sprouted black-socked toes from several holes. Oh good! She wasn't under-dressed!

The old house loomed behind him, and Rob Baxter had been right. It was hideous. And yet. . . The pale sunshine struck the age-greened copper of turret roofs the shape of circus tents and onion domes, and there was a huge pile of weed-matted slate in a corner of the jungle of garden which would make wonderful paving. The once luridly painted stucco had fallen in patches everywhere, too, to show clean, yellow-grey Yorkshire stone beneath, and she rather liked the fact that the house had all the symmetry of a child's clay model.

'It's incredible, Callum.'

'Yes, incredible to think that one man—and not a stupid man, at that—would try to pit himself in hand-to-hand combat with this monster.' His glance skated over her. 'Want to have a cup of tea, or something? Or get straight to work? You look. . .um. . .appropriate.'

'Oh, good,' she said drily. 'That was the look I was striving for. Appropriate. No, no tea.' She didn't want him to think that she was here only on the pretext of working. 'Let's get down to it while the light is still nice.'

There was a pause, then he raised his eyebrows. 'Keen!'

'Cold!' And scared, actually. She thought that she'd probably held a hammer once or twice in her life. She must have, surely? But she couldn't for the life of her think *when*, nor what she might have been hammering. But, as usual, this awareness of being under a handicap only squared her jaw and her resolve.

Callum took her inside, standing back a little as he opened the door, and she could see his unstated pride. Saw it, in fact, before she looked at the entrance hall she was standing in, and realised what he was so proud of.

'This is where I come when the rest of it seems like it'll never get done,' he said, and she took in the glistening expanse of polished floor, the newly stripped and stained skirtings, doors and window-frames, the pale, pale yellow of the smooth walls and the new power outlets, light switches and fittings. The sweeping stairway to the right, as well, was beautifully renovated, with a runner of heavy-duty Nile-green carpeting leading to. . .a cheap, roughly-nailed piece of board blocking the top.

He followed her gaze. 'Both floors upstairs are still untouched.'

Leading her through three beautiful big rooms, he then threw open a pock-marked and much-painted door to proclaim, 'The building site,' and she saw that the back half of the ground floor was still some way from completion. The floors were unsanded, with torn pieces of linoleum still adhering to the boards in places, loose wiring pushed out of holes in the walls and ceilings and naked plasterwork revealed just how much patching and sanding he'd had to do to restore the smoothness of the finish.

In the middle of the floor there was a heap of paint-splattered tarpaulin and he began to spread it out, anchoring it in place with pieces of slate which he must have brought in from the pile she had seen outside. She saw that the woodwork was all covered with newspaper and tape. 'We're painting today?'

That didn't sound too daunting. He nodded, then suddenly swore. 'The other roller! Damn! I got called in for emergency surgery the other day and forgot to put it in water. It's stiff as a board. So there's only the one now. Can I get you to work on something else?'

'Of course,' she said gamely. 'I'll do anything. Whatever needs to be done.'

'Really?'

'It's why I came.'

Ten minutes later she wished that she hadn't sounded quite so confident. She was a better actress than she thought, and had clearly convinced him that she knew exactly what she was doing. Alone, surrounded by tools whose names she didn't even know—let alone how to use them—she heard his heavy tread echoing as music swelled forth from the stereo system positioned safely out of the way in one of the rooms he had already finished.

The music resolved itself into the sounds of a folk-rock group, and when a woman's voice began to sing, Megan heard Callum join in with unselfconscious emotion and pleasure—a bold, full-bodied sound. She listened to him, heard his tread again and then a clatter and a squeak— the sound of paint cans being opened and a tray and roller prepared. Here, in the dingy warren of back rooms, she felt abandoned but it was all her own fault.

'These shoddy partitions need to be taken down,' he had told her. 'God knows how many poor souls the previous owner crammed in here. But it's a horrible job. Would you rather paint? Or I can drum up something else.'

'Is this what really needs to be done next?' she had insisted.

'Well, yes, it's what I'd planned. . .'

'Then I'll do it.'

But how?

OK, Dr Megan Stone, you're an intelligent woman and a top professional in your field. How hard can it be to knock down a few walls? She ticked off the tools on her fingers. Hammer. Well, the back end of that could lever up the heads of nails, or something, couldn't it? And what was this thing? A crowbar? Or a jemmy, perhaps. And a saw and an electric drill. She wondered with absent curiosity whether Callum had rewired this section of the house yet, or might she drill through a live wire and turn into a human lightning bolt? Hmm. Perhaps she shouldn't use the drill. . .

She could, of course, admit defeat here and now. Go back to Callum, who was now crooning the words of 'Matty Groves' in a voice that could have graced any stage, and tell him, 'I've never done this before in my life. Where on earth do I start?' But she didn't want him to think that she was some useless female with more enthusiasm than sense or, worse, that she'd only come in order to fling herself upon his manhood, followed by a free meal.

She did, in fact, want to fling herself upon his manhood quite badly, although she was terrified of the implications and the potential for pain, but there had been nothing. . . nothing she trusted. . .in that conversational duel over the issue of seduction the other day to convince her that he was still interested after all this time. He was a private man, and he could easily be involved with someone else. It was more than probable that coming here today would marginally increase her proficiency with power tools and that was all.

So—with that knowledge firmly in place—to work!

She picked up something that looked like Thor's hammer, gritted her teeth, squared her jaw and took an almighty whack at the middle of a piece of grubby and pitted plasterboard. Gratifyingly, when the dust settled, she was greeted by a huge hole. There! Not a useless female at all! As with any task, the application of brain power and common sense invariably reaped the desired results.

Enthusiastically she whacked again.

Ten minutes later, confidence soaring and plaster dust powdering her hair like snow, she faced a greater challenge. A big square post of solid wood—about as thick as Callum's arm—that had anchored the plasterboard in place at its junction with the original wall just wouldn't budge.

Jemmy, hammer, Thor's block-buster—each had proved unequal to the task. She picked up the saw uncertainly. It had a long flabby blade and wickedly barbed teeth, but when she tried to saw through the beam at floor level she couldn't get it to bite at all and the angle was impossible. Her hand kept getting bruised against the wall as she sawed the blade ineffectually back and forth.

Clearly radical surgery was not the answer, and it would be better to essay an exploratory procedure first. She picked up the drill tentatively. It was plugged in. She could see the portable power-socket board on the floor out in the passage, attached to a thick piece of orange cable which snaked its way out the back of the house. Now, if she used a broad drill bit—such as the one already in place—and made a couple of holes beside these big thick nails maybe she could then get a purchase on them with the hammer, and the beam—if it was called a beam— would come free.

She gave a tentative squeeze on the drill's trigger-grip. It whined, then died again as she let the trigger out.

'Well, that seems easy and safe enough' she muttered. 'If you let it go it stops.'

She listened for a moment. Callum was still ballading away in the other room. She smiled. So unselfconscious. . . But should she ask him before she tried this? No, on reflection she felt that she had correctly assessed the safety parameters, and that her diagnoses of problem and solution were correct. She positioned the drill carefully beside the big nail, perpendicular to the surface of the wood, felt a spurt of nerves and then overcame them in one bold squeeze of the trigger.

The drill screamed and bit into the wood then hit something hard, twisted in her hand and jumped back violently. Megan screamed, bit her tongue, hit her head on the beam—which was *very* hard—twisted on her feet and jumped back violently too. The drill wasn't stopping this time, although she'd released the trigger. What had she done? She dropped it, terrified that it would turn into some mad electric Catherine wheel, then stumbled backwards— straight into Callum's chest.

They were both knocked totally off balance. He just managed to wrench the drill cord plug from the power socket, then they fell together in a turbulent cloud of plaster to land in a heap on the floor. Slowly the drill whined into silence.

CHAPTER FIVE

THE dust settled eventually.

'Are you hurt, Megan?'

'I don't think so.' She was lying face down, pillowed on Callum's chest in a littered nest of plasterboard pieces. It felt. . .amazingly comfortable.

'What were you doing?' he asked.

'Trying to drill beside a nail. A big nail. In that beam thing there.'

'Drill beside. . .? Oh, you great idiot of a thing!' he crooned tenderly. 'You bloody fool! You silly lunatic of a woman!'

Lying there, motionless, watching the motes of the white dust drift softly down to snag themselves in the dark hair of Callum's forearm, Megan thought, If I could stay here like this in Callum's arms for the rest of the day, listening to him call me nasty names, I'd think I'd died and gone to heaven.

But, alas, that particular form of bliss was not to last. He stopped calling her names almost at once. 'I'm sorry,' he groaned. They were still both just lying there, not moving at all. She could feel his steady, controlled breathing, and hear the resonance of his words in his chest. 'It wasn't your fault. It might have worked if you'd had a steadier hand.'

'Why did it keep drilling when I let it go? It didn't when I practised.'

'The trigger has two settings, half-squeeze and a full squeeze. The full squeeze locks it on, then you push a button at the side to switch it off.'

'Oh.' Keep talking, I want to listen to your voice in

your chest like this, and watch your arms and feel your
thighs under mine. . . He shifted a little. He had one arm
around her, and it tightened. She felt the change in her
own breathing as her awareness of him increased.
Callum. . . Oh!

'Have you not done much of this sort of thing, then?'

'I've never used a power tool in my life.'

'Oh, Megan, you bloody idiot of a thing!' he groaned.
Those blunt, tender names again. 'Why didn't you say? I
was just coming to check on you when I heard you
scream. . . But if I'd thought you didn't know what you
were doing I'd never have left you alone in the first place;
never have given you this terrible job! You could have
painted! Why didn't you say, you great, silly—'

'. . .idiot of a thing,' she finished for him.

'Sorry.'

'No, you're right. I—I wanted to prove I wasn't
useless.'

He groaned again and she felt its resonance against her
full, tender breasts, transmitted through their soft clothing.
She could feel so *much* of him like this. There was silence,
and she thought weakly, hoping, almost aching for it, I
wish. . . I wish he'd. . . Kiss her. Hold her.

Then she heard him say carefully, 'Megan are you all
right now?'

'Yes. . .'

'Could you. . .get up, then, please?'

'Oh, God, sorry!' She scrambled off in an instant,
flushing.

'No, it's fine,' Callum said quickly. He turned from her
so that she wouldn't be able to see his face or the tell-tale
pull across the front of his jeans, and made a performance
out of brushing himself down. 'Had a piece of plasterboard
sticking into my back, I did.'

He still couldn't look at her; could have kissed her just
like that for. . .hours! Even with their mouths gritty with

plaster and tasting of paint. But he was so befogged with desire for her at the moment that any of the usual signals from female to male, if she was giving them, were a garbled mess across the emotional air-waves and he honestly didn't know. . .

Two years. Perhaps I'm just projecting all this. She certainly didn't come dressed to entice.

But it was amazing how good she could look to him in that baggy old gear. Get a grip on yourself, Callum. The last thing you need is a repeat performance of that madness two years ago. Take it slowly. . .if your body will let you. It was still clamouring, and he struggled with his breathing.

He's embarrassed, Megan thought. Did he guess. . .what I was thinking? Brushing her own clothing free of plaster dust, she said quickly and brightly, 'I made a pretty big hole, though, didn't I?'

He gave a shout of laughter, and an unnameable tension in the atmosphere dissipated somewhat. 'You did all this? In about fifteen minutes? How?'

'I just whacked with Thor's hammer there.'

'Thor's. . . The sledgehammer.'

'Yes. It wasn't even hard. You're right. The construction is incredibly shoddy.'

The tension eased a little more. 'On the strength of that. . .' he pointed at the demolished wall '. . .and this. . .' he threaded a large chip of plaster out of the hair that swung beside her neck and she suppressed a shudder of awareness '. . .I think you'd better come across to my place and have that cup of tea I suggested a while ago.'

'Come across. . . Isn't *this* your place?'

'Yes. I make myself a nice fresh plaster bed every night, with a paint can for a pillow and a tarpaulin for a blanket,' he told her drily.

'OK,' she conceded. 'I thought maybe there was a room or two with your things in it that I hadn't seen. So you have a flat nearby?'

'A flat? No! I live in the elephant house.'

She was totally bemused, of course, and he was, too, by her ignorance of his circumstances.

'I get teased about it at the hospital all the time. Callum Priestley lives in an elephant house.'

'I—we—we haven't exactly spent much time in each other's company, Callum. I've—not been around enough to hear people teasing you.'

'I suppose you haven't,' he said slowly and the tension was back again, thick and heavy, until he added hastily, 'Come and see what it's about, then.'

He led her out through the back door, leaving Fairport Convention still drumming away to themselves, and she could only follow him, still not sure what she expected to see. There was a wide brick ramp leading down from a strong, broad, stable door, and a similar ramp circled all the way up to the first floor.

He said, 'This house was built by a circus-owning family in 1891. They took the circus all over the country in spring and summer, and then in the winter months they lived here and quartered the circus animals. The smaller ones had special indoor pens at the back on the lower two floors. You see these ramps? Imagine them leading lions and bears up here! Now they'd make good wheelchair access—that's one of the strengths of this place as a home of some kind—and the elephants lived. . .'

He stood back to usher her through a jagged hole in the threadbare hedge at the back of the wild garden, and there was the elephant house. She gasped, delighted and laughing. 'It really was a house for elephants!'

'Yes. Three of them, apparently. Different ones over the years. The family closed their circus down in 1938 and, while the rest of the place was turned into that disgusting rabbit warren of illegal flats you got a hint of just now, this place was just left to rack and ruin. . .which saved it, really. Structurally, it was strong. I got in a work crew, and did as much as I could myself. It took four months to put in flooring and wiring and plumbing, and a bathroom and kitchen.'

She was still staring at the bizarre and oddly elegant little building. 'It looks as if some maidenly English cottage fell wildly in love with the Taj Mahal and this is their love-child,' she said.

He laughed, and repeated her own dry phrase of earlier in the afternoon. 'That was the look I was striving for.'

'Can I see inside?'

'Of course. We're having a cup of tea. Listen, though, did you bring your bag?'

'I left it in the house.'

'Does it have a brush in it?'

'No. . .'

'Wait here.'

He disappeared inside and returned a minute later with a man's wood-backed hairbrush. 'It's clean, I promise. I washed it yesterday. Now, bend right forward.'

She did, and saw the cloud of plaster dust herself as her fine blonde hair flopped in front of her face. Then she felt his fingers resting lightly on her nape, while his other hand wielded the brush in smooth, slow strokes. 'Your hair is such a silvery blonde,' he said softly. 'The dust almost doesn't show. But, oh, it's there. Close your eyes.'

'I am.'

He brushed a dozen more strokes in silence, then told her in his simple way, 'That's good now.' She straightened as he added, 'Mine's not nearly as bad. . .'

'But you need a hair-cut.'

'True!'

There was something quite intimate about the way he used the brush, straight from her own fair head to his so much darker one, and for a few seconds their eyes met and held as if he was thinking this too. Then he dropped his hand, holding the brush casually, and turned on his heel to lead the way inside.

It wasn't a very big place. The high, central onion-shaped dome rose over a comfortable living-room and the two slightly lower onion domes on either side had become a bedroom and a kitchen, both generous in size. Leading from the back of the living-room was a door then a small passageway to a bathroom, and it was in the passage that his two canaries sat in their cage with the diamond-paned windows and, in summer, the climbing pink roses in the background.

Megan was enchanted. 'You live in an elephant house!'

'I kept this big double door at the front,' Callum said, his enthusiasm very apparent, 'but I had to take the others down in order to put the wall and window in at the side. It used to be very simple and open, you see, just cement floors and the three big doors which they would have kept open in fine weather. This back bit, which I put the bathroom in and connected to the main house, was where they stored the feed.'

'I love it!'

'Most people do. Unfortunately, it's only big enough for one.'

'Well. . .two,' she amended, seeing the queen-sized bed which dominated the one bedroom, its head against the bright, diamond-paned windows.

'Two, I suppose. . .'

His green glance flicked past hers, and her breath caught. This was the bed where. . . The turbulent, erotic memories returned and she cursed herself for suggesting that two people could live here. She hadn't meant it that way, but. . . You great idiot of a thing! she chided herself inwardly, echoing Callum's phrasing.

He was in the kitchen now, putting the kettle on, and she had time to notice that he'd decorated the little dwelling in the same style as its exterior, creating a quirky and oddly pleasant clash between Oriental and utterly English.

Since his appearance and accent suggested the stereotype of a man who might choose football trophies and
shelves of home-recorded videotapes as decorating motifs,
she found the Persian carpet, the dresser display of bone
china cups and saucers and the botanical prints of fruits
and vegetables doubly intriguing. Then she found the three
large carved teak elephants, sitting on stands amidst a
jungle of potted plants, and laughed.

He saw what she was looking at and said, 'Saw them
in an antique shop window and couldn't resist, could I?'

'Of course you couldn't! Do they have names?'

'No, I've been trying to find out the names of the ones
that really lived here when the place was first built, but
it's not in any of the papers I've got about the house and
beyond that I don't know where to start. Well, I do. . .'

'Old local newspapers, with stories about the circus?'

'Yes, but I never manage to get to the public library.'
The kettle began to sing. 'Look, do you want to make the
tea? I'm going to duck out to the hardware shop before it
closes and get another roller or two and some brushes.
Then we can both paint. I should never have left you alone
like that.'

'It was my fault, Callum,' she insisted. 'I shouldn't have
let you think that I knew what I was doing.'

'You exude too much competence for your own good.
I assumed you must have cut your baby teeth on an angle-
grinder.'

'A *what*?'

He was gone for about twenty minutes, so she had plenty
of time to find some Darjeeling tea—it seemed appropriate—as well as pot, cups, milk and sugar. She was
scrupulous about not looking into any cupboards that she
didn't need to open. The casual way he'd just left her
there suggested a degree of trust and familiarity that was

illusory and she wasn't going to take advantage of it. . . partly because she so badly wanted to.

She was hungry to know more about him—the books he read, the cooking ingredients he kept in his pantry, the way his clean T-shirts smelled folded in their drawer in his bedroom. And, because she felt such intense curiosity, it somehow seemed wrong to actually look at anything, even the books—although to browse along those big twin sets of bookshelves on either side of the door that led to the little passage and bathroom was surely what any casual visitor had the right to do.

When he came back he was surprised to find her still standing in the kitchen, aimlessly turning the cosy-covered teapot in her hands.

'You haven't had yours, then?' He saw the two clean cups she had set out.

'Of course not. Didn't you want me to wait?'

'No. It'll be stewed by now.'

'No, it won't because I thought you'd be gone longer and I only just filled the pot.'

'You were supposed to relax. Have you just been stand-ing here the whole time?'

It did seem silly and she was almost as embarrassed as if she *had* been caught snooping into his drawers.

'What am I going to do with you? I'm not letting you out of my sight, I'm not, for the rest of the afternoon!'

This suited Megan very well. Far too well, which was not what she had wanted to happen in her more sensible moments. She had had the half-formed idea in the back of her mind that getting to know Callum Priestley better might gradually shatter that dark, sensuous set of memories she carried within her about the night they had spent together, and leave her safe from a strength of awareness which made her so vulnerable.

Somewhere in the man, as she got to know him, there had to be an antidote to the power of those hours, she reasoned. Chronically smelly socks, say. Or an obsession with obscure football statistics from forty years ago, and a tendency to tell crude, sexist jokes and jeer at her if she didn't laugh at them. That sort of thing. But, so far, it wasn't happening.

Instead, she was discovering a man who lived in an elephant house and listened to Fairport Convention and had a way of delivering insults that was so tender she'd exchange them for endearments any day.

I'm falling, she realised. Falling, falling into something dark and warm and far too huge to be safe.

They drank their tea and he teased her some more, asking if she'd ever painted a room. She was forced to tell the truth. Somehow Callum wasn't an easy man to lie to. 'No, I haven't.'

Laughter cracked his face again. 'You know, when you said you wanted to help. . .'

'You can send me home, if you like,' she suggested humbly. 'If I'm wasting your time. . .'

'You're not, Megan. . .'

'I'd. . .like to learn. It's ridiculous, in my position, to be so helpless with tools. It's such a stereotype. Blonde and empty-headed, and I've already vastly impressed you with the attention I pay to the details of running my car.'

'Yes, most chest physicians on the brink of getting their consultancy are empty-headed,' he agreed drily. 'I expect it was a tough career choice for you, wasn't it? Medicine. . .or posing on car bonnets in stiletto heels and a bikini.'

'Don't knock it,' she teased. 'I expect the fringe benefits of sitting on cars are excellent.'

So he taught her to paint and they finished two rooms, listening to a simple, pub-recorded CD called 'Home and Away' by Clive Gregson and Christine Collister, then Puccini's *Tosca* for a change of mood. They finished up with Clint Black and Wynonna Judd, and Megan told

Callum frankly, 'I can't *believe* your taste in music!'

He grinned. 'Is it terrible?'

'No, just *weird*,' she said. 'We've had British folk and folk-rock, Italian opera and now American country. Where's the common thread?'

'I like the unashamed emotion, maybe. And getting to sing along to all of it.'

'Oh. Of course. But you haven't been!'

'Embarrassed,' he admitted. 'Have been, under my breath, and in my mind.'

'Oh, *don't* be embarrassed, please!' she begged. 'I love your voice! Well, I mean, it's very good. You're good. You sound as if you should have been in the recording studio too, or the pub, in that live recording. I was listening to you before when I was out. . .um. . .knocking down the wall.'

'And yourself.'

'And myself,' she conceded. 'And I thought you were quite. . .uplifting.'

'Uplifting?' he groaned. 'Oh, bloody great! That's really an incentive to burst into song, knowing you're listening to every note and getting *uplifted*!'

'Oh, Callum, I didn't mean—It was meant to be a compliment!'

'I know. I know.' He relented. 'But, you know, it's like singing in the shower. Private. I wouldn't have done it before if I'd known you could hear so clearly.'

'And I wouldn't have said anything if I'd known it would put you off.'

Distracted from painting for a good ten minutes, they finally reached an agreement that he would put on Steeleye Span and start singing again, as long as she was on the opposite side of the room finishing off the brushwork next to skirtings and window-frames—and as long as she joined in.

But it was hopeless. They both went in fits and starts,

couldn't concentrate, forgot to paint, went off-key and finally laughed and gave up the attempt, letting Maddy Prior sing without their amateur assistance.

It was seven by the time the rooms were finished and the equipment cleaned and tidied away. And it was *cold*. They had opened the windows to keep the place free from paint fumes and now it was thoroughly dark outside and a chilly wind blasted through the house.

Callum had promised her dinner if she outstayed his cynical estimate of three hours and she most definitely had, even with the false start earlier, but she wasn't sure, now, if he had been serious. He hadn't mentioned it, and she certainly hadn't seen any evidence of cooking. He closed the windows, leaving just an inch of air coming through each one, and she started to consider some polite phrases for taking her leave.

The he said abruptly, 'It'll be warmer back inside. I put the wall heaters on high after our tea.'

'Oh, so you were planning—?' She felt awkward, afraid of showing too clearly how much she wanted to go back with him to that odd little place of his.

'Dinner?' He turned to her. 'I said I would. If you want it. But if you've made other plans, of course. . .'

'No, dinner would be nice.'

'I'm not much of a cook,' he warned as they crossed through the threadbare hedge again.

The air of the house struck deliciously warm on her icy cheeks and she shivered convulsively and wrapped her arms around herself. He saw the movement and she felt his heavy touch on her shoulder for a tiny moment. 'Sorry, I should have lent you another pullover.'

'No, I only got cold once we stopped painting.'

'Now. . .' He threw open the freezer and explained seriously, 'I believe in the factory approach to cuisine. I have approximately six recipes in my repertoire, and I have twelve oven-proof, microwave-safe casserole dishes. I cook great big batches of about four different things every few weeks, decant them into the casserole dishes and store them in the freezer. Tonight I believe your choice runs to Irish stew, spaghetti Bolognese or fish pie. . .and haven't I made them all sound appetising?'

'Irish stew sounds nice,' she said cautiously.

'Because you calculate that there's not a lot of margin for error?'

'Something like that.'

The appropriate casserole dish was revolving sedately in the microwave a minute later, and Megan was still listening to its hum with a degree of politely hidden scepticism when—in the space of seconds, it seemed—he had opened a very nice bottle of red wine, set out two different cheeses and Bath Oliver biscuits on a wooden plate, thrust a long, foil-wrapped stick of garlic bread into the oven— 'They ought to make these things ring-shaped so they'd fit in the microwave'—and emptied a Cellophane bag of supermarket greens into a glass bowl.

She began to suspect at this point that Callum wasn't a bad cook at all, merely one who believed in leaving time for other things. Her taste buds leapt into action and suddenly she was starving. They sat at the kitchen table after he'd poured the wine and she ate so much of the cheese and biscuits that he nodded sagely and said, making her blush, 'That's right, safer to fill up on that in case you can't stomach the rest. I think I'll do the same. Touch and go, my cooking. You see, I've never understood what the recipe book means when it says, "dredge the meat in flour".'

His expression of honest puzzlement was so exaggerated that she choked on her Bath Oliver, and only just recovered before his big hand arrived to beat her soundly on the back. 'I'm all right, Callum,' she gasped, and the hand withdrew.

Any lingering doubts about the stew soon vanished. It was hot and savoury and delicious, with piles of thick gravy, and she laughed and blushed again at his face as she reached for a third helping. 'It's the manual labour,' she explained.

'I don't think I'll be able to afford your labour again, I don't,' he told her. 'You're eating the wages of two qualified tradesmen!'

'Oh, you're horrible! First you convince me it's going to be inedible and then, when I actually like it, you try to shame me into stopping before...um...before I'm full.' She winced guiltily.

He sighed with heavy patience, and broke her off three more pieces of garlic bread.

Later, just as she noticed that the wine was three-quarters gone and decided that she ought to make a move to leave, he put on the coffee percolator and kept her prisoner there with such delicious coffee that she stayed another hour. It was after ten when another surreptitious glance at her watch told her that she really did have to stand up and make her excuses. Because if he thought...

If he thought, if he guessed correctly just how much she wanted to stay, finish the wine, talk, move to the couch, feel his big shoulder drift into contact with hers and then find that he'd turned her hungrily into his arms...

'I've really enjoyed this, Callum,' she said quickly.

'Yes, most of my guests like to get attacked by a marauding electric drill and cover themselves in fifty-year-old plaster dust,' he returned smugly.

'No, really...'

'Really, if you want to come again for more of the same... Perhaps I could rig up a defective oxyacetylene welder for us next time, and have a little light show?'

She choked, then managed, 'Seriously, though...'

'Really? Seriously?'

'Callum... Look, I would like to come again.' She said

it boldly, feeling her blush and the slow pounding of her heart. Because if I don't say it—if I don't try—I'll never know, will I. . .?'

She saw the flash of fire in his gaze but it disappeared so quickly that she thought, after all, she might only have imagined it, and his words were gruff and blunt. 'Well, it's nice to have the help.'

'If you don't think I'm skilled enough—'

'Megan, I'd love to have your help if you seriously want to,' he said slowly, 'but winter's coming on, and we have to tackle those awful partitioned-off back rooms next and the same upstairs. It's not going to be an easy job. Really, this is purely my personal madness. . .'

'If I start to hate it I'll stop coming,' she told him.

'OK. Next Saturday, then?'

They were both edging towards the big double front door, through which elephants had once come and gone. As aware of Callum as ever, she realised when they reached it, He sat all the way across the kitchen table from me tonight. He's not standing very close now. He's not going to kiss me. I'd better get the whole idea out of my head.

He opened the door and stood there, like a sentry or a medieval suit of armour, as she ducked past. 'Goodnight, Callum.'

'I'll walk you to your car.'

'Thanks.'

They crunched in silence across the overgrown gravel that flanked the big house, and she felt his reserve in the way his big body moved beside her. As she unlocked her driver's side door and slipped in behind the wheel all he said was, 'Thanks for helping.'

She drove away but, when she got to the stop sign at the corner, she couldn't resist looking back at the house through her rear-vision mirror. He had already gone.

*　　*　　*

'If you're looking for Mr Priestley, he's still in surgery.'
Cecily Stark's precise tones arrested Megan in mid-
corridor and forced her to turn. The secretary had a new
blue rinse in her hair on this Monday lunchtime, and it
emphasised the striking ice-blue of her eyes which, surely,
must sparkle with humour and warmth at times. The
woman had laugh lines around her mouth and eyes, yet
Megan had never seen her crack so much as a smile.

'No, I'm not looking for Callum.' She kept her voice
cordial and then, perhaps unwisely, tried to melt the frost
with some humour. 'I'm looking for the big tin of Earl
Grey tea I bought just the other day. It's not in the first-
floor kitchen and I'm wondering if it might have grown
legs and gone exploring up here.'

Mrs Stark's mouth set hard. 'I hope you're not suggesting that Mr Priestley has taken your precious tea!' she
said indignantly.

Megan surrendered the hold on her anger. 'Of course
I'm not! Good heavens, Mrs Stark! And if he had I
wouldn't mind. I'm sure he'd have planned to put it back,
or let me know.'

'Then you *are* accusing him?'

'I'm *not*! I'm just saying—' She stopped and saw the
blue eyes bulging with enmity. 'Oh, never mind!'

Turning on her heel, she disappeared into the second-
floor kitchen and searched the bench and all the cupboards,
finally discovering the tea behind a huge jar of a particularly noxious brand of instant coffee. Grasping it in
triumph and needing a cup of it quite a bit more urgently
than she had done five minutes ago, she breasted the
kitchen door—to find Mrs Stark standing there watching
her from the corridor, arms folded suspiciously. 'So! You
got it!' she said.

'Yes, and it's still almost full, I'm happy to say!'

'And how do I know that it's your tea in the first place?

It could be Mr Priestley's tea, and *you* are the kitchen thief in this building!'

'Oh, for goodness' sake!' Megan groaned, and brushed past Mrs Stark, too angry to bother any longer.

Back at her desk ten minutes later, with tea and a cottage cheese salad roll, she was still fuming, so when Callum himself poked his head around her open door she met him with a frown.

He must have just come from surgery, as he was still in the theatre clothing which went beneath the succession of gowns he went through in the course of a long morning, and he looked—if she'd stopped to fully take it in, which she didn't—more than a little drained.

'I'm glad to see you,' she began ominously.

'Yes.' He wiped a hand across his eyes. 'I wanted to let you know—'

But she ploughed on, 'Your secretary has just accused me of stealing your tea.'

'*What?*'

'And, if she can't make that charge stick, her fall-back position seems to be that I'm accusing *you* of stealing *my* tea!'

'Oh, damn. . .' he muttered with a hunted look.

'Callum, she makes it clear that she detests me and I can't demand that she change her opinion, but her bare-faced rudeness is beginning to get to me, I confess!'

'Damn!' he said again, kicking the door shut behind him and dropping heavily into the chair opposite her desk.

She loved having him there and wished that she had something to entice him to stay, other than the dubious offer of half a sandwich and a cup of contentious tea. It's so nice to feel more relaxed with him at last! she thought. She noticed his fatigue then, and was appalled at how much she wanted to smooth away the lines it made in his ruggedly hewn face.

'I'll speak to her,' he was saying decisively.

'Do!'

'I'm sorry, Megan, really I am.'

'Is it something I've done, do you know? Because I'd be happy to try and make amends, if it is. I hate being disliked so strongly, particularly when I have no idea why. I really can't think of any time in the past when I might have said or done anything that—' She stopped abruptly, seeing the dark flush that stained his face now.

'You didn't,' he said with authority. 'You haven't.' Now he looked uncomfortable. 'It's just that she. . .er. . . has a rather protective attitude towards me and she—' He stopped and gave her a suffering look, then summoned a touch of humour to soften the blow. 'She's been aware of a certain awkwardness in the air between us and has only one explanation, which is that you don't appreciate me at my true worth—i.e. my weight in platinum—and you therefore deserve to be verbally drawn and quartered.'

'Don't appreciate—! But Callum, I *do*! I mean—' She broke off. What did *he* mean? That somehow Mrs Stark had guessed the essentials of that time two years ago? How *accurately* could she have guessed them? It didn't bear thinking about, and Megan certainly wasn't going to press for details.

'It's all right,' Callum was saying quickly and decisively now. 'She's overstepped the bounds, and that's unacceptable. I'll talk to her. It won't happen again.'

'Good,' she managed. 'Thanks.'

And, since Mrs Stark's attitude had suddenly turned into an embarrassing subject, she was relieved when he said, 'I dropped by to tell you about the two procedures this morning.'

'Mr Swinnard and Mr Turnbull! Oh, was it—?'

'Much as we thought, I'm afraid. Surgery is out of the question for Mr Turnbull. He's got diffuse oat-cell carcinoma and I'd be very surprised if it hasn't metastasised well beyond the lungs.'

'Chemotherapy?' she hazarded uselessly.

He shook his head. 'Unless he wants it. I doubt it'd do anything significant to prolong his life and certainly, even to give him a tiny bit more time, you're looking at a barrage of drugs which will make him feel ill and miserable.'

'I know.'

'You'll have to talk about it with him.'

'He may want the chemo anyway.'

'Yes, he's aggressive about it now. He wanted me to "cut it all out on the table, young man, even if I've got half a lung left at the end of it".'

'I hope we can switch that determination towards enjoying the time he has left.'

'You'd probably like to be there when I tell him.'

'Yes.'

'Later today? When he's out of Recovery? I'll give you a ring.'

'OK, and, now, Mr Swinnard. Please tell me that was good news!'

'As good as it gets. It's a small localised carcinoma way at the top of the right upper lobe. I doubt very much that it has metastasised.'

'His tests so far have come back with excellent results.'

'So he looks like a good candidate for surgery and by removing that lobe I should remove the tumour and still leave him with a lot of lung.'

'Thanks, Callum.'

He left, turning down her tentative offer of tea, but she didn't take it personally, under the circumstances, and then at four that afternoon they met at Alfred Turnbull's bedside shortly after his transfer up from Recovery and had to tell him the difficult news.

In spite of some continuing drowsiness, he was brisk. 'Well, I'm not leaving a wife to mourn me. Addie and I were divorced fifteen years ago. Now, my grandchildren, though. . . Will I make it till Christmas?'

They answered his questions until he grew too tired. There would, no doubt, be more questions tomorrow, as well as a reaction—as the truth sank in—of anger and rebellion. Mr Swinnard was given his far better news then Callum said, as they stood in the corridor outside Surgical Ward Two, 'I'm off up to Children's to see Bhasa.'

'I saw her this morning,' Megan nodded. 'That sternotomy's not looking as good as we'd like, is it?'

'No, there's an infection brewing,' he agreed. 'I've stepped up the treatment on that, and I'll see if there's been any improvement yet. It's all your doing, of course!'

'I know,' she agreed humbly. The steroids she had pre-scribed and which had been essential if Bhasa was to survive the stress of surgery had to be tapered down gradu-ally, not abruptly discontinued, and they slowed the healing of Bhasa's dramatic chest incision, making it more prone to the infection that now threatened.

'Could she stand being titrated down to no steroids at all?' Callum wanted to know.

'I don't know,' Megan grimaced. 'I doubt it. She's had a couple of bad asthma attacks over the past week and, to be honest, I'm not absolutely sure why.'

'New brother?' he hazarded.

'She seems delighted with him.'

'I'm sure she is. Doesn't mean that it's not stressful.'

'Nor that she's not seeking extra attention, consciously or not,' Megan mused. 'You're right, Callum. We'll have to see what we can do. I'd thought of it and dismissed it, but I think I was wrong. Blame it on never having been presented with a sibling myself!'

He raised an eyebrow. 'Only child? Same here. . .'

And there was that flash between them again—a sort of recognition. Things in common that they hadn't yet begun to touch on. Things that she hoped, in spite of any sensible inner cautionings, they would touch on eventually.

Perhaps he was thinking of this too because he asked casually, although they'd be bound to talk again later in the week, 'Still up for Saturday?'

'I've invested in some work gloves and a head-scarf to keep the dust out.'

'I'm impressed!'

'Wait till you see me. The scarf is not exactly flattering!'

He opened his mouth as if to speak, then shut it again on a controlled breath, gave a goodbye salute and sloped away towards the lifts, leaving Megan to stand aimlessly for a moment—staring at a wall-mounted fire-extinguisher and trying not to wish too much that it was Friday today instead of merely Monday, with the whole week still ahead.

CHAPTER SIX

SATURDAY did come eventually, of course, and Megan appeared as promised at Callum's house and again the Saturday after that, while life went on at Camberton Hospital as usual, seeming. however, somehow more stimulating and meaningful than it had been for a while.

Bhasa's infection slowly cleared up and her incision began to heal. She was almost ready for discharge, and Megan had quietly asked both the nursing staff and Bhasa's parents to coo a little less over baby Prakash and focus on Bhasa's own life—her schoolwork, her puzzle toys and the swimming lessons she hoped to start in a few weeks' time. Without making the little girl focus on herself in an unhealthy way, this shift in attention had reduced her anxiety and stress and the asthma attacks had become measurably less frequent and severe.

Mr Swinnard had his surgery, and was thus far keeping his vow of no more cigarettes. He seemed chastened by the cancer scare and touchingly attentive to his wife. Mr Turnbull had also given up smoking and was doing everything he could to keep himself feeling well until Christmas, which had always been a favourite time for him. Megan, in close consultation with the hospital's palliative care team, felt that he would be granted this last pleasure before the inevitable end.

On her third Saturday visit to Callum's house Megan found that Rob Baxter must have had a twinge of altruism after all because he was there as well, with Ariadne Demopoulos in perky denim overalls and an attractive cherry-red sweater underneath. The two of them worked with violent enthusiasm for the first half-hour, moderate enthusiasm for another half-hour after that and then, with frank laziness, wandered across to the elephant house to bring back coffee and biscuits for everyone, taking an unlikely amount of time to return.

When the coffee-break was finished they pushed piles of debris round with brooms and dustpans for another twenty minutes in a desultory sort of fashion, and then announced that they were going to the pub.

'Don't want to stay for dinner?' Callum asked, but not as if he cared much either way.

'No, thanks, Cal,' Rob answered cheerfully for both of them. 'I'm not convinced we've earned it, are you, Ariadne?'

The pretty Greek doctor made a face. 'Haven't we? It's horrible work!' They were finishing knocking down the partition walls at the back of the ground floor. Then she added hastily, 'But, no, Callum, we won't stay. Thanks all the same.'

And they beat a hasty retreat. It was half past five, and Megan wondered miserably, Am I just making a fool of myself here? She'd stayed for dinner the previous Saturday, choosing the spaghetti Bolognese this time, and again they'd talked for far longer than she had planned and when she'd finally left at ten-fifteen he hadn't kissed her. Telling herself very firmly several times as she drove home that she only wanted to be friends with Callum *anyway* didn't do anything to sweeten her helpless disappointment.

She said rather quickly now, 'I won't stay for dinner tonight, either, Callum, if that's all right.'

'Course it's all right. You're not obliged to stay. You're not obliged to come at all.'

He had his back to her, using a heavy jemmy bar to prise a thick wooden strut away from the wall where it was fixed, and his words were punctuated by the piercing groan of old nails pulling free. He wore gloves as he always did, thick soft chamois ones to protect his surgeon's hands, and his black sweatshirt was pushed up to his elbows to show the thick rope of his muscled forearms.

She couldn't tell from his tone or his body language whether he was disappointed or relieved, then thought with a spurt of anger at herself, Stop being so adolescent, Megan! Of course he wants your help and of course he only wants you as a friend, but that's OK. You haven't done anything embarrassing, like grovelling at his feet and begging for his body, so what's the problem? And she was enjoying the task of wrestling with this big old place more than she had ever expected to.

Callum turned, weighing the big jemmy bar in his gloved hands, and his face was pleated into one of those brooding and almost frightening frowns he sometimes wore at the hospital. 'You don't feel that you've made some kind of commitment to this that you can't get out of, do you?' he said slowly.

'No, not at all,' she told him brightly.

'Come because you want to, Megan, not for any other reason.'

The words hung significantly in the air and she could only gabble, not meeting his eye, 'I will. . . I do. . . I'll come again next Saturday. But I have. . .other plans tonight.'

'Good. You need to relax,' he told her, and she was absurdly disappointed that he hadn't expressed regret. 'You look tight around your eyes sometimes—a papery sort of look as if you don't let go enough.' He reached a hand out as if he was going to brush her face, then looked down at the thick, dust-powdered glove and left the gesture uncompleted. Megan felt the tiny puff of a sigh escape her. 'Anyway, let's get cleaned up, then, shall we?' he said.

Half an hour later she was at home in her flat alone, thinking too longingly of Callum's elephant house and wondering if he was having fish pie tonight—or if he'd had a cooking bee during the week and replenished his stocks with chicken curry, macaroni cheese and moussaka instead. These, she had learned, were the other dishes in his repertoire, and she had every reason by this time to think that they'd be delicious.

On impulse she checked her own fridge and pantry and confirmed that she would be able to whip up a quiche and salad then phoned Carol Bernard, the physiotherapist at Camberton Hospital who dealt with the cystic fibrosis patients that Megan treated. Since they met up with each other fairly frequently Megan knew that she was recently divorced, recently arrived in Camberton and rather lonely.

Carol was only too definitely free for the evening. 'Far freer than I'd ever want to be at the ripe old age of thirty-six!' she confessed drily, so the two of them ate quiche, gossiped and even managed a late movie.

But when Carol suggested that she reciprocated with supper the following Saturday night Megan said hastily, 'Could we make it Sunday?' and seven days later there she was pulling up outside Callum's house at exactly ten in the morning, wearing another stunning ensemble— jeans as old as Callum's and, atop two soft wool-blend spencers, an ancient man's shirt that came almost to her knees.

They were starting on the upstairs rooms today, with more walls to knock out, and had decided to make a full day of it. Callum wanted to get this dusty and filthy job done with before winter arrived in earnest, when opening the windows wide to clear the air would become a real penance.

It was pretty unpleasant work. Two weeks ago Callum had been studiously gallant about Megan's pink floral scarf, which she'd twisted turban-style on her head to hide every strand of hair, and he had approved of the new gloves, too, after inspecting them. 'Soft but strong. . .like their owner!'

'If that's a dig about my muscles. . . Just don't leave me alone this time!'

'Leave you alone? I'd wondered about handcuffing you to my wrist for your own protection!'

But, in fact, she considered that she was actually getting quite good at this—until she caught him watching her after they'd been at it for about half an hour and trying not to laugh.

'What's the joke?' She was indignant.

He warded off her fierce expression with exaggerated terror. 'No joke! Honestly! You've got a swing like a council labourer. It's just your face.'

'My face?'

'You get this. . .expression. Your mouth is jammed so tightly shut that you get dimples in your chin.'

'OK, that's it! The sledgehammer is yours for the rest of the morning. I'm just going to mince around, picking up a few bits of debris here and there in between painting my nails and cooing over your manly physique.'

'Now, Megan. . .!'

'No, sorry! You had your chance.'

They wrestled over the sledgehammer for several minutes, until they were both laughing so hard that it was dangerous, and finally settled back to work in a talkative mood which somehow led to mutual confidences about why they had become doctors and what had influenced them as children.

It was flippant and funny at first, and then it wasn't and he suddenly said, 'My mother left us when I was ten months old.'

'Callum. . .!'

He struck a piece of wall with the sledgehammer to punctuate the statement—not violently, but simply because it was the next thing he needed to do. Megan was sweeping up the debris several feet away and dumping it into an enormous green plastic garbage-bag of industrial strength. 'I think it was because I'd started walking, and she couldn't keep up,' he quipped. 'I was a pretty active toddler, I'm told.'

'That must have been—' She was appalled.

'Better than if she'd waited a few years. I've got no memories of her, which helps in a way. Never saw her again until we were told that she'd died, about six years ago, in London. Cirrhosis of the liver. She drank terribly. I think perhaps I was better off without her. My dad drinks a bit, too, but not like that. He did a pretty good job with me.'

'He worked, presumably. . .' She pushed a pile of plaster pieces into a bigger heap.

'Still does. Fitter and turner. Still in Newcastle. Had to leave me alone a lot after school. I was all set to start getting into trouble but then, when I was eight, I met Miss Binns.'

The way he said it, his voice and his virile face softening, made her say lightly, 'And it was love at first sight?'

He grinned and pounded at the wall again. 'Pretty much. She was my teacher, a neat little maiden of a thing; couldn't tell you how old.'

'Kids can't, can they? I remember when I was about six my mother told me she was eighteen, and I believed her. I believed her for years, and she let me. It was only when I got to about fourteen that I woke up to things and thought, Hang on a minute, Mum, you *can't* have had me when you were twelve!'

'You never talk much about your parents,' he accused, stopping and leaning on the big handle of the sledgehammer for a moment.

'Oh,' she drawled, 'Let's not get onto that sordid subject yet. It's just another case of alcoholic neglect. I want to hear about you. . .' he nodded slowly and there was that unspoken recognition again that they shared some quite unlikely things '. . .and Miss Binns.'

'Oh, Miss Binns. Well, she must have been perceptive about children. Perceptive about me, anyway. She could see how my face lit up when we did science experiments and one day she invited me to her house so we could do some more. And I loved it. I was hungry to learn when it was presented in the right way. I started going round there three or four times a week and if she ever got sick of me she never let it show.'

'Of course she didn't get sick of you! You were probably the light of her life!'

'I hope so, because I certainly cost her enough in food. I was tiny for my age, back then, but—'

'Now, Callum, *that* is an impossibility!'

'No! Dad wasn't much good in the kitchen. We just made do with odds and sods most of the time. I still remember that feeling of being hungry when I woke up in the morning and still hungry when I went to bed at night. So when I started getting two suppers—one dodgy one from Dad, and one delicious one from Miss Binns— it helped. She was the one who taught me to make Irish stew. . .and who got me interested in medicine.

'When I got to my teens I wasn't so interested in going to see her any more, and that was when Dad came into his own. He's blunt, Dad—rough at times, but he makes sense—and he made me see how cruel it would be to forget about her after all she'd done. Well, I didn't always like going—you know how selfish and intolerant adolescents can be—but I went, and I kept on going until I found her on the floor one day with a broken hip.'

'Oh, Callum. . .'

'She'd been lying there for eight hours, and if I hadn't come that day. . . Anyway, she had to go into a home after that and I visited her there, too, until she died when I was seventeen. And she must have liked me, I suppose, because she left me four thousand pounds in her will.

'It made the difference between medicine being totally

impossible and being. . .just a bit of a struggle, and if this white elephant of a place—' this time the blow of the sledgehammer *was* violent in intention '—ever turns into anything, I hope it will be the Adelaide Binns Home for— Ouch!' He'd dropped the sledgehammer on his foot.

'. . .Terminally Over-ambitious Surgeons?' she suggested.

He muttered dire things under his breath.

'Have you got any pictures of her?'

'Somewhere. Just a couple. A classroom shot, and a posed studio thing.'

'You could get a portrait painted from the studio one and hang it in the main hall.'

'That's an idea. . .'

They worked in silence for a short while, then he said quietly, 'Can you tell me about yourself, Megan?'

'Oh, me. . .'

'Fair's fair.'

She struggled with her reluctance for a tautly stretched minute then said, 'Well, does that line about work being the curse of the drinking classes mean anything to you?'

'Oscar Wilde, or someone. . .'

'Think so. Anyway, it fitted my parents to a T. It was a jolly nuisance to the poor things to actually have to go out and bring in money when they would rather have been drinking in idleness—which was the life they considered they'd been brought up to—and I was the icing on the cake of life's inconvenience. Oh, *Megan* has to be taken to the dentist. *Megan* needs new shoes. *Megan*, the sulky little nuisance. Mummy's got a pounding head, you horrid child; can't you shut up?'

'You got shunted off to boarding school, I suppose?'

'No, I was supposed to, of course. I would have preferred it, in all honesty! But they mucked it up somehow. Didn't get around to putting me down, or missed the scholarship exam. I mean, anything involving paperwork or organisation went to the four winds in our house. The bills lay around for months. . . Maybe they just couldn't afford it. I was never told straight out, except that there was always a hovering suggestion that it was my fault.

'So, no, I went to the local grammar school, which didn't help them to keep up the appearance of class, and then I got told I wouldn't be allowed to stay on for A-levels unless I paid my own way. ''You've already cost us enough, you ungrateful little prig.'' So at sixteen I got a part-time job as a ''nasty little shop assistant'' for twenty hours a week, on top of school, and then got shouted at because I was too tired to clean the house—*Don't* insist on more details, Callum. . .'

'Of course not. Sorry.' They had both stopped working. He was watching her, his face twisted with a mix of anger and compassion and understanding.

'No, I did want to tell you,' she said, trying for a briskness which didn't quite come off. 'The essentials, anyway. . . And then, about five years ago, a great-uncle left them just enough money to retire to the south of France, la-di-da, where my mother suddenly discovered she was a thwarted artist. My father, not to be outdone, is now ''a writer'', and both of them maintain that lots of cheap red wine assists their struggle with the muse. Or muses.

'I—haven't visited them for nearly three years, and they never come home. Neither of the visits I did make seemed to inspire much in the way of parental happiness.'

'Megan, come here.'

'Hmm?'

'I said, *come here!*'

But he didn't wait for her to come and with two of his big strides she was in his arms, feeling him hold her— trembling at the touch of him, the way his arms wrapped around her, the shielding expanse of that chest where she laid her head and the gentle caress of his hand against her cheek.

'I hate hearing you talk like this,' he groaned. 'I bloody hate it! Your voice and your face go all hard and brittle, especially when you try to make it funny, and your body loses its grace. It reminds me of how you used to look when you first came to Camberton.'

'How I used to—?'

'So determined. *Too* determined. Brittle as china, as if one tiny mistake would kill you, and as if you were running a marathon and the finish line read ''Consultancy'' and you wouldn't stop once until you got there.'

'I did, though,' she told him. He had released her again, his arms dropping suddenly as he stepped back, and she wanted to pull him to her again.

'I know,' he said.

'I was due to take my final exams and I cancelled them a week beforehand.'

'I know.'

'How?' She didn't dare to reach for him. That big body was too self-contained, as if he regretted having held her at all. If she touched him and he pulled away. . .'It wasn't much talked about,' she managed.

It had been about a year ago and she'd indefinitely postponed going for her FRCP because if she was terrified of failing then she was even more terrified—a startling realisation, this—of *passing*: of being committed once and for all to an ambitious career path along which she could see no time for the other parts of herself which she had neglected so badly for too long.

'How?' he echoed. 'I asked Tony Glover. You looked different suddenly.'

'*Oh?*'

'Better. I didn't see that brittle look in you again until just now, and I feel bad because I made it happen—because I made you talk about things that you hate.'

'No. Don't. I—I'm glad that you know some of it. It sounds trivial, but—'

'Trivial? You were abused, Megan!'

'Abused?'

'Do you think it has to be physical?' he demanded. 'Do you think it has to come in a working-class package? *My* sort of package? A crummy little house, and nowhere to play but the street, and Dad giving the kids a whack after he's been too long at the pub?'

'Did your father. . .?'

'No, my dad didn't. Not really. Nothing worse than a strap or two.' Which was whacking as far as Megan was concerned! 'My mum would have, by all accounts, if she'd stayed. Perhaps that's why she left.'

They talked about it some more—carefully, thoughtfully, painfully. Different stories, each of them had, and yet there were links and she knew that she wouldn't regret her honesty with him, as she might have done if he'd known only a thoughtless happiness in his childhood. She sensed that he was more forgiving of his father than she might be if she ever met the man.

'Total waste of a morning!' he said finally, in mock disgust, when they each looked at their watches at the same moment and found that it was ten past twelve.

She laughed. 'Please, sir, I'll stay late to make up.'

'You certainly will!' he threatened. 'Let's eat now, then, and do a better job this afternoon.'

So they sat outside on the ramp at the back, where it was sheltered enough to give some warmth to the unexpected November sunshine, and ate the thick sandwiches he had made earlier, washed down with Thermos tea. They didn't say much as they ate, which was a relief, somehow, after the intensity of this morning's talk, and it felt so comfortable that she took another sandwich just to prolong the quiet pleasure of their silence together.

But it wasn't possible to prolong a sandwich picnic on

a November day for ever. Callum got to his feet, screwing the paper wrapping from the sandwiches into a tight ball, and Megan followed him into the house. Back at work, though, with some deliciously tawdry American country music playing and their beepers side by side in the corridor out of reach of the dust, they hadn't even struck a single blow to the plaster when both instruments began to pipe within seconds of each other.

They exchanged sinking looks and he took off the gloves he had put on seconds earlier.

'I'll use my car phone,' she said quickly.

'Same here. I'm virtually never paged unless they want me to go in. It must be serious. Brian Pelham's on today and he doesn't panic over nothing.'

'And I'm usually only called in if it's one of my own patients,' she told him. 'It seems odd that both our beepers went off at once. . .'

They separated at the back ramp of the house, as Callum kept his car in a small yard behind the elephant house. Her own car was parked at the front, a greater distance to walk, and she heard him speeding away just as she unlocked the driver's door. And by the time she reached the hospital he was already in surgery with a race to run against death. . .

Her own role was less clear and less technical, but not necessarily less hard.

'Where's Gary?' she demanded of Casualty's Charge Nurse, Daniel Jones.

'Bouncing off the walls somewhere around here.' The tall, thin man grimaced expressively. 'We couldn't get him to sit down, or have a cup of tea or anything. He's very, very distressed and just kept asking for you or Julie Stebbins, the nurse from his cystic fibrosis clinic. I couldn't reach her so I paged you. I hope you don't mind.'

'Of course I don't! I've been seeing Gary during his

hospitalisations for four years. My God, he was my first patient at Camberton!'

It was just three and a half weeks since Gary's last stint in hospital had ended, and Megan knew that physically he had rebounded well and was as fit as anyone could hope for at the moment. This, though, was very different from his usual problems.

'Go and look for him, then,' Daniel Jones said.

'I will. First I'm going to get the full story from you, if you've got time.'

'Brief run-down, OK?' the charge nurse said, eyeing his busy department. 'Gary and two friends were working on a car, and they didn't have it properly jacked up.' Knowing what she was about to hear, Megan drew in a hissing breath as Daniel gave the rest of his concise, clinical summary of the crush injuries.

'So they're both in surgery now, one with Callum Priestley and Brian Pelham and the other—Peter Salmon, the crushed leg—with Ted Laycock and the rest of his orthopaedic team.' He broke off and focused over Megan's shoulder. 'There he is, coming back through the double doors now. I told him you were coming in and he must have been looking for your car outside.'

'Thanks, Daniel.'

She hurried towards the small, slightly built nineteen-year-old, and felt her throat catch as she saw his face and his stance.

'Dr Stone!' he croaked, bringing his hands up in fists against his gut.

'Gary. . .' She tried to hug him, aching for him, but he fended her away.

'Don't, I've got car grease all over me.'

'I'm not exactly dressed up myself!' She showed him her old jeans and shirt, but he was too upset to smile.

'You heard what happened?' he demanded. She could hear the wheeze and rattle in his lungs.

'Yes, but not much detail. Tell me, Gary.' After everything his CF had put him through, she hated to see him like this over something that wasn't related to his disease at all.

'It's crazy!' he moaned, dead white. 'It's wrong! *I'm* the one who's supposed to die! I've been preparing for death my whole life and my life's probably three-quarters over, and now, useless me, I'm not under the car when it happens and those two who should live till they're eighty. . .' He choked and pressed the back of his hand to his mouth, then started coughing thickly.

'Are you all right, Gary?'

'I skipped my physio this morning,' he admitted.

'Oh, Gary. . .'

'We wanted to get a good start on the car. Mum had to go to work. And then *this* happened, so I've missed my lunchtime session as well. Mum doesn't know about the accident yet. But what does physio matter. . .?'

'It matters! Let's do it now,' Megan suggested decisively. If she could calm him by resorting to a familiar and vital routine. . .

'What? Are you daft? My friends are—'

'Your friends are with two of the best surgeons in the country. You can't see them or do anything for them now. You've only just got yourself fit again, and you can't afford a set-back now.'

'Why not?' he said bitterly. 'Now seems like a great time for a set-back then I can join Chris and Pete in hospital. . .if they make it.'

'I will not let you talk this way, Gary!' She almost manhandled him over to Daniel Jones, and asked the charge nurse, 'Is there a treatment room we can go to?'

'Yes, take your pick down the end, but—'

'Gary missed his thumps today. We're going to do them now. Come on, Gary!'

If the charge nurse thought that there was anything odd in this he didn't say, and a minute later Megan had Gary using his inhaler then settling into the first of nine positions in which she would rhythmically thump different sections of his chest and back to reach every part of his clogged lungs systematically. He was far more familiar with this procedure than she was, and took up each position with a blank resignation which worried her.

She asked him several times, 'Is this hard enough?' but he only nodded absently, and when she deliberately tapered off the force of her hands he didn't comment until she prompted angrily, 'Gary!'

'Yeah, OK, harder. Much harder, if you like. It works better hard.'

Finally, after fifteen minutes, she said, 'There!'

'There's two positions I usually do myself now.'

'OK. Good. Do them!' Megan could see that his pounding action was half-hearted at best, but didn't push it. 'And do you have your inhaled antibiotic on you?'

'No.'

'Don't forget to take it at home, then.'

'Mmm. . .'

'I'll ring you to remind you, OK?'

There was no answer.

'*OK?*'

'OK.' He shrugged.

'Now, what about lunch?'

'Haven't had it.'

'Then—'

'I'm not hungry.'

'I'll take you up to the cafeteria now.'

'No. . .'

'Gary! Look! What can I do about this? It *wasn't* your fault!'

'If they die. . . Maybe they're dead already and no one's saying. *You* know, and you're not saying because you don't think I can take it. *Poor sweet little Gary!*' he mimicked cruelly in falsetto. 'He's a CF patient, Gary Henley;

he's had *such* a hard time—better protect him from the truth as long as possible. Don't *lie* to me, Dr Stone!' He swore then was seized by a fit of coughing, which was so violent that it left him shaken and exhausted and clutching at the painful muscles of his abdomen.

'Come on,' she said to him as soon as the paroxysm was over and he had recovered his evenness of breath.

'What? Where?'

'I'm going to feed you. . . Then *prove* to you somehow that your friends will be OK.'

She was pinning her faith blindly to Callum in hoping that she *could* prove it, because Chris Kennedy's chest had been badly crushed, apparently, as well as his neck and jaw, and she couldn't know for sure that he would survive. Peter had an extensive but not life-threatening crush injury to his legs.

Gary took the barrage of enzyme capsules that most CF sufferers needed with each meal in order to digest their food properly, but his appetite was understandably poor. Megan let him get away with a small bowl of soup and a bread roll, but knew that if this guilt and anger over his friends' accident didn't resolve itself soon then he would be risking a major downturn in his condition through lack of commitment to the constant, demanding routines and safeguards that were a part of his life.

Megan was still at a loss as to how to act to push him through this, and couldn't forget his mimicry half an hour ago. She had understood for a long time that mollycoddling Gary only angered and alienated him, and tried not to fall into this way of relating to him herself. Gary respected her for it, trusted her, she thought. But when the crunch came, like today, he was suspicious.

I've got to prove to him that I'm being straight with him, she thought.

She thought of Callum, immersed in surgery—remembering how she had watched him over four weeks ago during Bhasa Singh's surgery—and suddenly an idea came to her.

'Come on,' she told Gary in the blunt tone to which he responded best.

'Wh—?'

'You're not going to start on that sandwich, are you? You've just been staring at it for ten minutes. Bring it with you, if you like, and let's go.'

'Where?'

'I want to show you what's happening to Chris.'

It was quite a distance from the cafeteria to the hospital's suite of operating theatres on the top floor, and the journey—along covered walkways, down corridors and in the lift—gave Megan plenty of time to face the risk she was taking. If the surgery was going badly... If Chris *wasn't* OK...

For a moment she almost changed her mind, but realised that if Chris wasn't OK then this was the best way for Gary to find that out too.

They reached Theatres. She was relieved to find that Anne Dashwood was on today, and drew her aside to say, 'Can you find a gown for Gary, and one for me?'

'You're taking him in? Who is he—a med student? Dr Stone, Mr Priestley said—'

'Not a student. The owner of the car that crushed the two lads in surgery now. The one who was lucky enough not to be under it at the time.'

'Oh. Good Lord! Then—'

'He's one of my CF patients, Anne,' she pleaded. 'This is unorthodox, I know, but he's got more than a case of guilt here. He thinks it should have been him, because he's "dying anyway", and he thinks we're lying to him about the other two. And, whatever happens later on, if he doesn't see this I don't think he's going to trust us, and I don't know how we'll get through to him to motivate him to go on living.'

'To go on living? Not suicide, surely?'

'Yes! Passive suicide! What could be easier for a CF patient? Simply slack off on all his routines and drugs, and he lays himself open to an infection that could kill him in weeks. Certainly within the year.'

'Take him in, then,' Anne agreed. 'It's a madhouse, though. They've called in a microsurgeon for the Salmon boy to sort out the nerves in his legs, and a jaw man is coming down from St James's to reconstruct Chris Kennedy's face. He'll be here any minute. Meanwhile, Mr Priestley is getting ready to hand over to the orthopods to tape up his chest and shoulder.'

'We'll watch through the windows. I don't think we'll need to go in. Thanks, Anne!'

'He's your patient.'

'I know. I'm responsible. If there are any complaints or queries, direct them to me!'

'They're in Theatres Three and Four.'

'OK.'

She took the gowns Anne had provided, as well as mask, cap and shoe covers, and helped Gary put them on, saying little beyond what she needed to in the way of terse instructions. Along the corridor Theatres One and Two were dark and not in use, but Theatre Three was hectic with activity.

'That's Peter. They're working on his legs,' Gary croaked.

'Yes. That's Mr Laycock there, with the grey hair and glasses, and that's Grant Mayhew, the microsurgeon.'

Gary nodded and watched in silence for several minutes. 'So he won't lose his leg, then. . .' he said, half to himself. 'If it couldn't be saved they wouldn't be working on it like that, would they?'

'I doubt it.' She didn't tell him that the hours of microsurgery could yet fail to restore the limb's full function.

'Where's Chris?'

'Along here.'

They reached the big window of Theatre Four and there was Callum still at work, repairing the terrible damage to the young man's lungs and heart. Megan recognised the junior general surgeon—Brian Pelham—who had called Callum in, as well as Ben O'Day—another top-notch orthopaedic surgeon—who would do what was needed to Chris Kennedy's crushed left shoulder.

Gathered around the garishly lit table, Ron Rose, three nurses and an orthopaedic registrar added to the sense of crowding. Megan saw that blood was being transfused rapidly into a vein and wondered how much Chris had lost.

It was an intimidating sight, even for someone like Gary who had seen so much of the inside of a hospital, and for some time he just watched the silent pantomime of surgery through the glass while Megan watched him.

'Pretty serious, isn't it?' he said finally.

'Yes.'

'But they're not doing that frantic stuff with defibrillator paddles and whatnot.'

'No, it's very focused, careful work—this sort of surgery.'

'They're repairing him, like we were repairing the car.'

'Yes.'

'Who's the big bloke?'

'Callum Priestley. Cardiothoracic surgeon.'

'He's seen us. . .'

Megan realised it at the same moment, catching the quick glance from Callum above his mask. He looked down again at once, his focus fully on the inert body in front of him once again. She and Gary might have disappeared, for all the awareness he showed of their presence.

'How much longer will it take?' Gary wanted to know.

'A good while, I should think.'

Although Anne Dashwood had said that Callum should soon be finished. And, yes, even now he was stepping aside to let Brian Pelham take over. He watched for a moment, said something to one of the nurses, then backed away from the table and pulled off his gloves, dropping them into a bin before coming towards the door. Still capped as he emerged into the corridor, he had loosened his mask to let it beard beneath his chin. His black brows communicated a question to Megan.

'This is Gary Henley,' she said quickly. 'The one whose car they were working on. He needs to know that Chris is going to be all right.'

Would Callum understand just how much he needed to know it? She wished that she could have taken him aside and told him about Gary—his CF, his guilt and anger, his need for strength and honesty and directness in the professionals he dealt with. But there was no opportunity for this now.

'Gary,' Callum said. 'Good to meet you.' He held out his hand, and Gary squeezed it convulsively.

'Tell it straight, please, Dr Priestley.'

'Straight?'

Megan nodded, a tiny movement that she didn't want Gary to see, her gaze fixed on the darkly fringed wells of green that were Callum's eyes. Straight, Callum, as straight as you can make it, please!

She saw his tiny nod in return, and then he spoke. 'Chris is badly injured,' he said bluntly. 'I can't promise you anything yet. Everything has been done, and is being done, and we think he's going to live.'

'*Think?*'

'Didn't you want it straight?' he demanded.

'Yes!'

'I'll tell you one thing, though,' Callum continued in his darkly masculine voice. 'He wouldn't be alive now if it hadn't been for you.'

'But it was my car! I should have been under there too.'

'And then both of you might be dead. . . Because it was

your pocket knife, too, wasn't it? And you who made that slash tracheotomy in his throat, and your ballpoint pen, as well, that you took the middle out of to produce an open breathing tube to slide through the hole you'd made.'

'What else could I have done?'

'Bloody hell, Gary! If you *hadn't* done it—bypassed that blockage in his airway—do you think he'd have lived long enough for us to get our hands on him in here?' the surgeon demanded, seeing Gary's reluctance to accept his praise.

'Gary, you didn't tell me this!' Megan said incredulously.

'I thought that charge nurse would have told you. I mean, what else could I have done?' he repeated. 'It was a nightmare, and if I hadn't been so. . .' He swore. 'So *stupid* with that jack and those bricks Pete piled up—'

'Oh, Gary!'

She was practically shaking him, as Callum said bluntly, 'How the bloody hell did you know you needed to do a drastic procedure like that? How the hell did you know *how* to do it? You're not a medical student, are you?'

'I have CF,' Gary said simply. 'I know about breathing! Actually doing it was pure guesswork, but I knew I had to try.'

'Well, your CF saved your friend's life. Is that straight enough for you? It took a hell of a lot of courage on your part to do what you did, so if you're feeling guilty about this, my advice is, don't!'

'Chris's mum and dad. . .'

'Are in for a rough time. I'll make sure they know what you did. It was heroic, Gary, OK? And I don't use that term lightly!'

His glance was fierce and powerful for a moment then he looked beyond Gary and raised his hand in a brief salute, and Megan saw that a man dressed ready for surgery was coming along the corridor towards them. It had to be

John Buchan, the jaw and face specialist who had come down from Leeds.

'I'll have to go,' Callum said. 'But if I hear another squawk of guilt. . . Gary, you're going to be busy for a while. Chris needs you. Peter too. Guilt is a poisonous waste of time, OK?'

He glared again, didn't wait for an answer and stepped forward to greet his colleague.

Megan took Gary aside. 'Have you seen enough?'

'Yes.'

'I hope Mr Priestley wasn't too—'

'He was bloody marvellous, actually. Just bloody, bloody marvellous,' Gary said shakily.

CHAPTER SEVEN

IT WAS another half-hour before Megan left the hospital. With a new strength and maturity in his voice, Gary had said that he wanted to go and find Chris's and Peter's parents and stay with them until there was more news. He wanted to phone his mother too. She would be home from work by this time and, no doubt, very alarmed.

Megan met the two sets of parents, fearful that she might have to step in if Gary became too distressed at seeing them. In the end, though, he dealt with the situation well and Megan told the story of the emergency slashing of Chris's throat, stressing the speed and courage of Gary's response and proud of the latter's handling of the Kennedys' shaky and tearful thanks.

As she drove away at last the shadows that brightened and faded beneath a now-blustery sky were lengthening, and she wondered what to do with the rest of the day. It was an anticlimax after such drama. She'd been expecting to eat at Callum's tonight, too. . .

Then it suddenly occurred to her that there was no reason why she shouldn't go back to the house and work there on her own for a while. They hadn't packed up the tools. They hadn't even locked the place, if she remembered rightly.

She grinned as she thought of Callum's face if he came back in a quarter of an hour and found her there with another partition demolished. It would be a little lonely working there on her own, but he really shouldn't be too much longer and she could put on music for company. She'd then be able to hear an up-to-the-minute report on Chris and Peter when he arrived.

There was a party going on at the house across the street, and cars had filled all the available spaces in front of the old circus house. Megan cruised down the lane at the back to look at Callum's parking spot, but it was too small to fit two cars so she ended up in a little side-street some distance off.

Eager to shake off the mood of the hospital and to pass the time quickly until Callum's return, she put on lively music straight away and went upstairs to the windowless room they were ready to start on next. The day was closing in, and she had to hunt for a light switch before she could see whether the sledgehammer was already there or not. Finding the switch at last and flicking it, she realised that the bulb must have blown. At that moment the door, blown by a strong breeze from the open window opposite, slammed shut behind her.

At once it was completely and very unpleasantly dark and she had to grope her way back to the door, seizing the old-fashioned doorknob gratefully and twisting it quickly. And twisting it. And twisting it—to find that it just moved loosely around, to no effect at all. Had it simply become unscrewed? She twisted some more, hoping desperately that it would begin to tighten—but it didn't and she had to accept, after a frantic few minutes, that the thread was stripped.

'This is idiotic!' Speaking aloud didn't do much to stem a rising sense of panic. Five minutes ago everything had been going fine, and now. . . That was the way accidents happened, as with Gary's car today. 'There has to be a way to get this door open!'

There wasn't.

Several more minutes of blind groping in the dark, rattling, kicking and feeling for a latch or a snib or a hole or a key—*anything*—forced her to accept this fact. She could hear the music faintly from downstairs and it reassured her but there was something ominous and

frightening about having to get down on her knees to feel
around for the sledgehammer, desperately hoping that it
was there and that she could bash her way out.

Covering every inch of dirty floor twice, disorientated
in the darkness, she finally had to accept that it *wasn't*
there and she slumped on the floor, hearing the pounding
of her blood in her ears. She said aloud, 'Callum has to
get here pretty soon! I'll just have to wait.'

The music downstairs stopped after about twenty more
minutes, and it was like a friend leaving without saying
goodbye. She felt bereft then heard footsteps and laughter
and was on her feet again, her mouth opened to call out,
when suddenly she stopped.

That wasn't Callum. Who on earth was it?

She heard more laughter, raucous and wild, and she
thought, People from the party across the street. They're
very drunk, from the sound of their laughter. And, after her
childhood, it was the kind of sound she knew rather well.

'Watch it, mate, there might be someone here!'
she heard.

'Nah! There'd be lights on.' It must be quite dark outside
now, but Megan remembered that she'd arrived when it
was still bright enough to see well without lights on the
ground floor.

'Let's put them on and take a look round. . .'

'This is a weird place. . . Hey, look, there's a CD
player.'

'Let's nick it, and get out of here.'

'What's your hurry, Mike? Let's take a good look at
this place.'

'Hey! Look at this bird with the knockers and the feather
headdress. . . And this one; what is it—*opera*?'

There was a brittle plastic clatter. They were looking at
the CDs. Megan recognised the description of one of the
sopranos featured on the cover of a Puccini opera. There
was more laughter now and echoing sounds as the two—

hopefully just two—drunken party-goers roamed around the house.

She was torn in two. Should she call for help? It was the obvious thing to do, and the prospect of rescue was so sweet, and yet. . . Those voices didn't sound very pleasant. Straining to listen, she was desperate to hear something that would convince her that she could trust them but it didn't come. Instead she heard the crash of broken glass and a slurred voice saying, 'Let's just take the CD player and get out before someone comes, Phil. What's the point in tr—. . .in sh—. . .I can't say it. . .*smashing* the place?'

'Cos it's fun?'

'Yeah, and the CD player's worth a couple of hundred pounds. I'm taking it. You stay and throw bottles, if you like.'

'Get knotted, Mikey.'

'Yeah, and you get—'

There was a long, crude swearing match that eventually ended in more laughter, and Megan made up her mind. The prospect of being released by these people now seemed far more dangerous and unpleasant than the predicament she was already in. Silence on her part, then, and a fervent hope that Callum's arrival would chase them away. If they decided to come upstairs, and saw her leather bag slung just outside this door. . .

'OK, Mikey-boy, you're right. Let's just knock off the CD and not spoil the poor bloke's *luvverly* paintwork.'

'Take the CDs too?'

'That junk? I wouldn't listen to it. Couldn't even sell it, do you reckon?'

There were more footsteps and the odd comment, less distinct now. Megan thought she heard, 'No, leave the speakers. Too big.'

Then a door slammed and there was silence, and she dared to believe that they'd gone and she was safe. From one peril, at least. Now, if Callum came, saw her car and realised that she was here; saw the lights left on and came in to find her, calling her name. . . Her ears almost hurt from listening, and her breathing was tight and high above her knotted gut.

Another hour passed. . . More! Or did it only seem that long? She was getting very cold, and started pacing the room just to keep warm and occupied. Since she didn't have her bag containing her car keys she couldn't even use one to begin scraping a hole in this shoddy plasterboard. If her stomach was any guide it must be after six by now. Her thoughts became blacker by the minute, and she remembered what Callum had said a couple of times about sad lives lived out here in the illegal bed-sits. She wanted to shout and hammer on the door, but if those louts or their friends were the only ones within earshot. . .

Although even they would be welcome now, she began to think. Was she a fool to have stayed silent in here and let them get away?

Was that the music of the party across the road that she could hear? The party. . . She suddenly remembered—her car wasn't parked at the front where Callum would see it as he drove past to reach his back lane. And had Mike and Phil left the lights on or off? She tried to remember what they'd said on the subject; tried to think back to any sounds she might have heard which could have been the old-fashioned pull-cords at the back of the house clicking on or off.

If the lights were off Callum would have no reason to think that anyone was here. And he'd be exhausted by now after the hours in surgery. It was hardly likely that he'd come in here again today to work. Tomorrow. . .?

'I could be in here all night. . . Could I possibly make a hole in this wall with my fingernails. . .?'

A dry sob of near-hysteria rose in her throat, then she stifled it as she heard a sound downstairs and blood beat so hard in her ears that she almost couldn't hear. Was it

Mike and Phil, returning in search of more booty? Some of their friends, perhaps, even drunker now?

Footsteps. Slow and cautious. Her impulse to scream and call for help was so strong that she had to grit her teeth to keep quiet and insist to herself that a night or more alone and trapped in here was still preferable to being attacked. The footsteps again. Were they Callum's? Oh, please God, let them be Callum's.

Why didn't he speak? Because he was alone and had no one to speak to? It *must* be Callum, then. Or had Mike or Phil returned alone? She could tackle one man, perhaps. . . She kept listening. The footsteps stopped. Utter silence again. Had he gone? Who *was* it?

And suddenly she couldn't stand it any longer, and was calling on a sob of fear and despair, 'Callum? *Callum*? Is that you?'

The footsteps again, drumming in the direction of the stairs. '*Megan*?'

Oh, God, it *was* him!

'Callum! I'm upstairs. I'm trapped!'

His tread pounded now, and she was trembling at the prospect of release. 'I'm here! The room we were going to start on,' she called. 'The doorknob's broken—and the light!'

Seconds later he'd wrenched it open from the other side and the bright light from the corridor, which would have hurt her dilated pupils, was blocked by his bulk. She stumbled into his arms. He held her—so warm and solid— and she sagged against him, listening to his heartbeat and the vibration of his voice in his chest.

'What happened? There's glass smashed all over the floor down there, and the CD player is gone.'

Incoherently she sketched out the story and almost sobbed as she finished, 'I was too scared to call for their help. I thought they might hurt me. I just sat here and listened to them stealing your CD player, Callum, and when they'd gone I didn't know. . . I thought I might be stuck here all night. I'm sorry. . .'

'Sorry?' He was incredulous.

'I could have tried to stop them if I'd called.'

'The only thing you shouldn't have done was come here alone.'

'I know.' In hindsight it had been foolish. 'I was expecting you much sooner.'

'I had to go back into surgery. He went into cardiac tamponade and we had to open up his chest again. One of those crushed ribs had speared a vessel but we found it all right, and now he's looking good. Then I spent quite a bit of time with the parents, and stayed to check on Chris once he was settled in the ICU.' He drew away a little, just enough for her to see his granite-like face— moulded into very sober lines. 'He's still on the critical list but my instinct is that he'll pull through, and if he does survive this initial trauma we've put him together well enough that there'll be almost no long-lasting damage.'

'That's. . .wonderful! What time is it, then?'

'About seven. God, Megan! You've been in here for over four hours.'

'Am I a silly great idiot of a thing again? I feel it. . .'

'Yes! No. . . Hell!'

He pulled her closely to him again and she sighed raggedly, then gasped as he turned her face upwards with shaking fingers and kissed her—his mouth pressing hungrily and clumsily against her face until she fully understood what was happening and stretched to give him her lips. He was so warm, and she realised that her own mouth must be icily chilled. She could scarcely control its movement at first, but then his knees softened and warmed her so quickly that the numb clumsiness disappeared and she returned the pressure of his mouth, touch for touch.

Two years ago the dark whirl of their night together

had opened a world of sensation for her that she had never experienced before, and she had thought then that it was as perfect as two people could be together physically. She had been wrong. She'd known so little of Callum back then. Now. . .

I love him, she acknowledged in bewilderment. This is what love is.

This mix of passion and warmth and utter safety. Knowing him, yet so hungry to discover him. In his arms now she gave herself to him more fully through a single kiss than she had that night two years ago when she had given him her entire body, and her hands crawled over him—aching to rediscover the precious shape and feel of him that she had known so briefly and with such a disastrous aftermath.

His fingers stroked her neck, threaded their way through her silky hair, ran like a waterfall down her back and then came round to engulf her own hands in his warm grip.

'You're so cold, Megan,' he groaned, his mouth against her hair. 'Let me take you home to my place.'

'Yes. . .'

He seized her icy hand and they clattered down the stairs together, so close that they almost stumbled. In the rooms painted just a week or two ago, she saw the litter of broken beer bottles and said on a sharp hiss of breath, 'All that glass!'

'Forget it,' he growled. 'It's not important now.' Then he switched off the lights and locked the door, and they fled out into the darkness. He took her hand again.

The elephant house was a haven of warmth and so were his arms as he turned immediately to hold her again, chafing his hands along her shoulders and arms—taking her hands to say, 'Still like ice.' He lifted them to his face and kissed them. 'This is no good. . .'

Pulling them down again, he lifted the front of his black sweatshirt and thrust them inside. She felt the convulsive shiver he suppressed at their chilly touch against his chest, then shivered herself as she registered the feel of him— the hardness of that warm shielding wall, the silky roughness of its hair.

'There. . .' He sandwiched her hands between their two bodies as he stroked her back. Still against his skin, her hands slid around his torso and she just wanted to hold him and feel his lips on her hair; let herself savour this, school her urgency. Had he meant that kiss to happen a few minutes ago? she began to wonder. How much did he want it? Could it possibly matter as much to him as it did to her?

He sensed her new stillness and became still himself, to say questionably a moment later, 'Megan?'

'I—'

'Should I stop? Apologise?'

'No.'

'Then. . .what's happening? I'd begun to think that all you wanted was to be friends—God, it's an insipid word in the wrong context! And I—But surely that's not right! Surely there's much more!'

'No, I don't think we're just friends, Callum,' she whispered intensely. 'I can't be just friends with you.'

'No.'

'I want. . .'

'Yes. For four years. . .'

'I want. . .' She sighed against him, too scared to say it even now.

'I know what you want,' he growled.

'Oh, Callum, can we pick up—? Start again?'

'Where we left off two years ago?'

'Yes.'

'I was beginning to think you'd never ask,' he said lightly, and then they didn't talk any more for a long time.

*　　*　　*

They made love beneath the stars. She didn't realise the fact until the first heat of their passion had subsided and they were tangled together beneath the downy quilt on his big bed. Looking up into the dark canopy of the domed ceiling, she saw the celestial panorama and laughed aloud—intrigued and disbelieving.

'*Stars*, Callum? Not a glass ceiling. . . No, surely not!'

The stars glowed greenish and still, like chips of diamond and tourmaline on black velvet.

He laughed as well. 'Do you think it's daft? It's just a couple of packets of glow-in-the-dark stick-ons. They don't show in the daytime because the ceiling's painted cream. There was a chart of the constellations included so I mapped them out as closely as I could to the real thing.'

They both kept looking upwards. She was pillowed on his upper arm, and the hand that snaked around her waist drifted up to lazily stroke the sensitive weight of her breast. She gasped. . .and he held her fullness in his palm, touching his lips teasingly to her ear.

'It's wonderful,' she managed. 'The stars, I mean. Not daft at all. They glow for a long time, then?'

'Not really. It's not all that long since we turned the light off.'

No indeed! With the damask curtains pulled across the windows, they had begun their exploration of each other in the soft glow of two bedside lamps and she shivered as she remembered the so-recent image of his nakedness and virility, unashamedly displayed to her as he stood beside the bed, like the model for some classical sculpture.

The lamplight had glowed on the contours of shoulders and buttocks, and cast dark shadows across his chest against the heavy weight of his manhood. She had been naked by then, too, having stood—hypnotised by his tender, heated touch—as he'd pulled off the man's shirt she wore and bent hungrily to the fullness of her breasts that thrust softly beneath the two fuzzy wool-blend spencers. These had been quickly dispensed with as well, along with jeans and the inconvenience of underwear and shoes, and then they had fallen to the bed together.

The light had been part of their pleasure. She tingled, thinking of the way his gaze had caressed her breasts before he'd touched them. Then, when he had touched them—stroking and cupping, bending his dark head to nuzzle her, lifting their weight to his lips—she had watched the way his almost reverent pleasure had softened his virile face.

Later, as she'd held him and felt the thrusting acceleration of his need, she'd closed her eyes, lost—adrift on a turbulent sea of ecstasy—then had opened them again to glory in the sight of him—the granite-like face which had blurred because it was so close to hers, and the hot ripple of his back as he moved. It was only when they'd each washed up on the calm shore of fulfilment which followed the storm of their love-making that he had lazily reached over and switched off the lamps, to hold her while they both dozed a little in each other's arms in the darkness.

And now, a timeless, quiet interval later, opening her eyes to find stars. . .

She watched them while he said lazily, 'That's Orion, up there, and the Great Bear. The comets are a bit of artistic licence.'

'Yes, I should think so. Six of them!'

He nuzzled her ear again, his hand still cradling her breast, and said, 'Hungry?'

She thought about it for a minute. . .poor tummy, having to battle against the cacophony of signals from every other nerve-ending in her body. 'Actually, yes!'

'We'd better have something to eat, then.'

So, lazily, they began to dress. Spurning undergarments, Callum put on his black sweat-pants and -shirt again and Megan slipped into silky briefs then reached for her matching bra. He stopped her, taking it out of her hand, and picked up the spencer—pressing it between them as he pulled her close and whispered, 'Just this, Megan. It's warm in here. . .'

And the knowledge that he wanted to let his gaze linger on the soft, blurred contours of her breasts as they ate together, here in privacy, made her melt with both the memory and anticipation of desire.

She nodded breathlessly and slipped the spencer on, feeling the slightly scratchy softness of the wool-blend knit against her passion-grazed nipples and fully aware that his eyes were on her. If he reached to touch her again. . .

But they *were* hungry. In the kitchen he rummaged in the fridge for pâté and cheese and butter, found a bag of lettuce and jars of artichoke hearts and olives and tossed them onto the coffee-table as they were—too impatient for elegant serving. Then he heated lentil soup from a tin in the microwave and served it in big bowls and splashed wine recklessly into two glasses as well, so that in minutes they had an untidy feast prepared and ate it, lolling and lazy, on his comfortable couch.

Megan dripped a tiny splash of soup onto her skin just above the low, rounded neckline of the spencer, and was aware again of the soft garment's semi-transparency. Her nipples made dark, rounded shadows beneath and she saw, with a rolling pleasure, how often Callum's gaze was drawn to those dusky circles. It wasn't a one-sided thing. Her vision was equally caught and held by him—the way the resilient fabric of pants and sweatshirt stretched and softened over muscles and sinews as he reached for more bread or cut wedges of cheese.

Her happiness was so intense that she was almost afraid to breathe, let alone to speak, and perhaps he felt the same because he was very quiet too, just telling her a little more about the afternoon's crucial surgery and how he expected Chris Kennedy to progress over the difficult weeks ahead.

'That reminds me,' Megan said, 'I have to ring Gary.
I said I would—to remind him to take the inhaled antibiotic that he missed after his midday thumps. I'd like to
grab a talk with his mum, too, if I can.'

'Better do it now, then,' he suggested.

'Oh. . .?'

'It's after nine already, and you'll be busy for the rest
of the evening. . .won't you?'

Her breath caught in her throat. 'I—I hope so.'

'You will, Megan, believe me!' And his voice was dark
with a threatening, intoxicating passion.

And so she went out to the phone on the wall in the
kitchen and talked to both Gary and Mrs Henley. Things
sounded better than she had hoped. He had taken his
enzyme capsules and eaten a good dinner, and was about to
submit to his mother's experienced hands for his evening
chest-pounding routine. Cathy Henley reported, 'He's
upset. . . He's going to sit with Chris and Pete as much as
he can. . . But it's right for him to be upset. This was hard.'

Callum was clearing away the meal as Megan finished
on the phone and she gasped then laughed as he trailed a
long kiss across her neck and collar-bone on his way to
the fridge, with cheese and pâté and half a bottle of wine
juggled expertly in his hands.

'I've got to say, Megan,' he told her in a suffering tone
when she put down the phone, 'I'd never realised thermal
underwear could be so bloody erotic.'

And she had never realised that a man's gaze could be
that way, too, that it could feel so good to be so openly
and unashamedly desired by him. As Callum watched her,
having returned from the fridge, she felt her shadowy
nipples harden and peak against the loving cling of the
knit fabric, and when he lunged across the room to catch
her up in his arms she arched to meet him, glorying in
the path of heat that he kissed from her shoulder to the
soft cleft between her breasts.

'Dishes can wait,' he muttered. 'Megan, can I. . .get you into bed again?'

'Oh, please. . .'

In the dark this time, so that it was all touch and taste and sound. First he lifted the spencer up beneath her arms to hold and cup her breasts once again and she shuddered convulsively at this touch and pressed forward, eager for more of him—eager for his lips there too. He gave her this pleasure, then undressed her fully with feverish impatience and pulled off his own clothing. She heard the soft noise each garment made as he flung it to the floor.

Then the bed sighed and groaned as it took the sudden onslaught of their weight and, somehow, they ended up with his head pillowed against her belly, so he seized the chance to kiss each inch of her skin from her navel upwards until at last—quite a long time later—he reached her lips.

There he stayed for minutes until his kiss seemed to fill the whole of her awareness—the centre of a spinning pool of sensation which encompassed the silky chafing of his chest hair against her breasts, the hard weight of his thighs on hers and the total intimacy of touch low across her torso.

When he filled her at last she took him in her arms and gathered him more closely against her with her legs, feeling that there could not be a better way to show her love than this. Then she went beyond even this achingly physical thought and could only feel. . . Feel the climbing peak of their rhythm, the convulsive clutch of his hands across her back and the groans that were wrenched from him in musical harmony with her own cries of release.

They slept almost at once, warming each other without the need for a covering, until hours later when the heating had switched off and one of them, three-quarters asleep, must have pulled the feathery quilt up to form a toasty cocoon. Megan slept more soundly than she had done for months, and woke to a sound that she realised at last was the canaries chirpily heralding the late dawn.

Callum was awake too, his big torso half-pulled from the warm quilt as he watched her and his face softened yet hard to read. He murmured lazily as he saw her eyes open and focus. 'Still here this time, then?'

She blushed and said in a low voice, 'Yes, I'm still here. Of course I am!'

'Sorry. . .'

'No, if I hadn't run away before then perhaps. . .'

'No regrets!' he ordered. 'You're here now. Are you staying for breakfast too?'

'If I'm invited.'

But she knew that she was. There was nothing but clinging, relaxed warmth in this 'morning after'. He was touching her now, gentle fingers tracing loopy circles on her shoulders in a way that made no demands. She propped herself up on one elbow and just looked at him, drinking her eyes' fill of that arresting face which somehow *shouldn't* have the power to make her heart flip giddily like this.

And suddenly one of the most powerful phrases in human language crowded against her lips, and her heart hammered as she thought, I want to say it. It's true. I want to say it so badly but I don't dare, in case. . .

Bloody hell! Imitating his own blunt idiom, she schooled herself and felt the bite of tears behind her eyes. I have to be able to say it because I have to see. . .what it does to him. And before she knew it, the words were spoken.

'I love you, Callum.' The words were terrifying when they echoed in her head but as soon as they were said they felt so right that she said them again tremulously, tasting them in her mouth like a creamy sweet, 'I love you. . .'

Her heart thudding as she searched for his response, she saw the flash of green fire in his gaze and then his sudden, rough-hewn smile. 'Welcome to the club!'

'Wh—?'

He buried his face in her neck and said gruffly, 'Megan Stone, I've been in love with you for four years.'

'Four *years*?'

'It's been a bloody nuisance, most of the time, to be honest!'

'You can't have been,' was her blunt response. 'You *can't* have, Callum. It's barely four years since I came to Camberton.'

'Yes, and I met you on. . .I think it was your third day. Another stubborn patent ductus arteriosus, like the one we saw a few weeks ago. James Bradley.'

'No, it was a girl who had it a few weeks ago. Sally Morgan.'

'Yes, but four years ago the boy's name was James Bradley.'

'You remember his *name*? After four years?'

'And I came into the NICU and saw you, looking down at him and frowning at his chart, with this, "I'm an extremely intelligent and incredible doctor," look on your face, battling with a look that said, "This baby is so tiny I'm afraid he'll go into respiratory arrest if I so much as blink." And you looked so sophisticated—and so bloody beautiful—in your. . .let's see, navy suit with the candy-striped blouse. . .?'

'You remember my *clothes*?' And where were my eyes? Where was my brain and heart back then? she wondered, because I don't remember him that day at all. I must have been completely blind!

'And yet your face was so tender,' he was saying, 'and your voice was so tender when you said his name. "Baby James," you said. "Little baby James. . ." And I thought, I don't care who she is, or who *I* am, or who she's with. . .'

'I wasn't with anyone. I was, well, a mess, really.'

'. . .I want to hear her say *my* name with that sort of tenderness.'

'Callum—'

'There! Like that! Naked like that too—with your hair in a mess over one side of your face, and propped up on your elbow watching me, with your lovely creamy breasts spilling so heavily against my—' His breath caught and he broke off then said huskily, as the twin forms he had so sensuously described began to tingle and swell in response, 'And it's taken four years. . .'

'You're shaking, Callum,' she managed, knowing that she was too.

'Four years is a long time.'

'Is that why you're shaking?'

'Yeah, and with bells on! I was really thinking that it was never going to go away, let alone do me any good. And what happened two years ago only whetted my appetite, made me distrust myself, question a physical desire so strong it could make me take advantage of—'

'You didn't. I did. Didn't we have this conversation a few weeks ago?' she said ominously.

'Maybe,' he growled. 'I've lost the ability to think straight at all when it comes to you. As I said, it's been. . .' his breath caught again '. . .a bloody nuisance.'

She lunged for him and he caught her in his arms and she was so overwhelmed by the blunt emotion of his words that she just lay there, burrowing into him and feeling her own heart beating and the shallow pant of her breath, as she thought, I'm scared. Can love really be this good? Why me? Why didn't someone else grab this fabulous man ten years ago? He talked about marriage once and said it was greater than the sum of its parts. That's how I feel now. This is bigger than me. Can I live up to it? To what he's just told me? What if, when time passes, he's disappointed. . .?

But thought was swept away and made impossible as his kisses pressed hungrily into her hair. A moment later he sought her face and she slid up to meet his mouth with hers, feeling in full, exquisite detail the way their bodies flowed together in a gentle friction.

'Your lovely creamy breasts,' he murmured again, 'and this pale silky hair, and these shoulders that try to be much stronger than they look. . .and succeed. And these lips— the way the top one gets a bit fuller than the lower one when you're uncertain of yourself.' He nipped at each one lightly, then caressed the nip away with his tongue. 'And these rounded shapes down here, and these thighs. You've made life sheer hell for me, Megan, and if this is real. . . if I'm not dreaming. . .'

'You're not,' she whispered. 'And I'm not. Oh, Callum, make love to me. . .'

And, for a delectable hour, he did.

CHAPTER EIGHT

'WE'LL want to extubate him as soon as possible, of course,' said Jim Allyson, the rather cocky young registrar, who sat beside Chris Kennedy's bed. 'So, to that end, I'm adjusting the ventilator settings now; starting to wean him off.'

He turned to the machine, and thus did not see Megan's raised eyebrows and Callum's set mouth. The latter asked blandly, 'And why exactly do we want to extubate him as soon as possible?'

Jim Allyson looked surprised. 'Well, I mean, we just do. It's the current thinking, isn't it?'

'Dr Stone, as a respiratory specialist you've probably got something to offer on this issue.'

'Er, yes. . .' She blushed and knew that he'd engendered it deliberately with that absurdly formal seeking of her opinion, at the same time barely managing to keep the secret, sensuous glint in his eyes from erupting. into a frankly wicked grin.

Jim Allyson frowned and looked at Megan, while the rather starchy ICU ward sister, Martha Pomfrey, stood by and waited for these interfering and space-consuming doctors to get out of her way. It seemed impossible that neither Jim nor Sister Pomfrey were aware of the steamy atmosphere between the two senior doctors. Megan felt as happy and replete as a cat stretched out in the sun after a fresh-caught meal, and if she *could* manage to keep from looking at Callum it certainly wasn't for long.

But this was Chris Kennedy they were looking at, and nearly sixteen hours after he had come out of surgery he was still listed as 'critical'. Not a patient who warranted a routine set of instructions. He was hooked up to the ventilator that Jim Allyson wished to rid him of, and was rendered almost oblivious to his surroundings by pain medication.

A pulmonary artery catheter was taped to his chest, as well as an arterial line, and several peripheral IV lines snaked along his limbs. He had a Foley catheter and the odd-looking, white compression stockings which prevented deep venous thrombosis.

He had been seen several times during the night by Jim Allyson, who was covering the ICU, as well as by Brian Pelham. For some time longer he would be 'specialled' around the clock, receiving one-to-one nursing care from experienced staff such as Sister Pomfrey, until his condition showed significant improvement.

Megan studied his chart, noting medication and other details, then said to a rather suspicious-looking Dr Allyson, 'I wouldn't try and extubate yet, actually, and I wouldn't change the ratio on the ventilator.'

'But we don't want to blow up his lungs too much.'

'You may have to. With his injuries, what's too much for part of his lung may be not enough for somewhere else.'

'It's not a simple equation, Jim,' Callum cut in. 'If we compromise the cardiac output. . . He has an increased need for oxygen and we have to provide it.'

'Not to mention the pain medication, which is going to depress his own breathing mechanism,' Megan said.

'Make sure you do a haemodynamic profile for me as soon as possible, showing the cardiac output, oxygen delivery and oxygen consumption,' Callum said with deliberate pomposity, and Jim Allyson looked a little alarmed.

As the registrar turned back to his machinery and papers Megan caught Callum's dry smile. So did Sister Pomfrey.

'That should keep him busy,' Callum murmured to the

ward sister as they moved away from the patient's bedside and stood just outside his door.

'Hope so,' Sister Pomfrey drawled.

'Do keep him out of trouble, if you can,' came the surgeon's growl. 'He's too big for his boots with this "latest thinking" on ventilators and whatnot. Now, over the last few hours. . .'

Martha Pomfrey gave a concise and expert report, and Callum nodded.

'Everything pretty much as expected. I'll be in again late this afternoon to see him but meanwhile, of course, you'll page me if you need to.'

'Very good, Mr Priestley. And you, Dr Stone?' There was a faintly accusing note in Sister Pomfrey's tone. Clearly she wasn't quite sure where Dr Stone fitted into this patient's treatment. She was a thoracic physician, and while she could advise on respiratory problems following trauma and surgery she rarely did. The way her department's workload at Camberton Hospital was usually divided Tony Glover or visiting Fellow Nathan Fleishman were the ones to be called in to the ICU if a thoracic physician's input was necessary.

Typically, Callum rescued her. He was outstandingly good in that role, she considered, remembering his appearance in the doorway of the black hole she had been locked in last night. 'Dr Stone's concern is more with this lad's friend,' he explained easily. 'Gary Henley is a long-term cystic fibrosis patient of hers and the course of Chris's recovery will have important ramifications for Gary, emotionally and possibly physically as well. She's anxious to be able to give a first-hand report, and to make it good news if she possibly can.'

'Gary Henley,' Martha Pomfrey frowned. 'He's been asking to see Chris, and he's seen the other lad, apparently. . .'

'Yes,' Megan said. 'Peter Salmon's condition isn't nearly so serious.'

'The order at the moment is for one member of the immediate family at a time, and no friends as yet.'

'Keep it that way,' Callum advised. 'Megan, I'm happy to talk to Gary about how Chris is progressing, if you think that would work.'

'It'd work,' Megan said decisively. 'He was very impressed with you yesterday. Thought you were "bloody marvellous".' And so do I, said the creamy smile she couldn't manage to repress. She grew hot as she saw the flash in his green eyes that she now recognised for what it was—a desire in him that she hadn't dared to hope for until now. 'But I can't ask you to take that time. Gary is my patient, and I'm in contact with him and his CF clinic on a regular basis. It's easy for me to drop in here and keep up with Chris's condition.'

'If you'd prefer, Dr Stone.' He was back to the formal approach again but then he ran a hand very deliberately down her back to her thighs, almost under Martha Pomfrey's nose.

'I—uh, yes.'

'If I see him, though, I'll make a point of stopping to talk for a minute.'

'I'm sure that would help.'

'Just what is the problem with the Henley boy?' Sister Pomfrey interposed, a little irritable now as she clearly sensed that there was *something* she was being left out of here. If only she knew!

'He feels he's to blame,' Megan said, 'as it was his car.'

'Although, from what I understand, all three of them were responsible for jacking it up so badly and not even on level ground. . .which, ironically, is what saved their lives as it fell a crucial few inches to the side,' Callum said.

'When Chris's visits do extend to friends Gary should be the first one allowed in, then,' Sister Pomfrey suggested.

'Definitely! As long as Chris is happy about that. It will help Gary enormously to know that he has a role in speeding up Chris's recovery,' Megan answered. 'Forgive me for seeing things in my own terms but, in its way, Gary's condition is just as critical as Chris's, and it would be tragic if we lost control over his CF because of something like this.'

'I understand,' Sister Pomfrey nodded. She gave a watery smile. 'It's amazing what ramifications we have to keep track of, isn't it? I'll make sure that what you've told me is written up in the patient's notes. And now I must go in and—'

'Watch Dr Whiz-kid?' Callum suggested drily.

'Exactly. . .'

Sister Pomfrey ducked back into Chris's room, as he was due for his next round of observations and needed suctioning and mouth care as well. Jim left, looking a little chastened. Watching the senior nurse's experienced, caring actions for a minute or two, Callum murmured, 'Don't know why it's the surgeons who get the god-like status. I couldn't do that work, so constant and intimate.'

Megan looked at him in surprise as they left the ICU. 'You're not supposed to say things like that,' she accused gently. 'You're a heart-lung surgeon. You're supposed to be revoltingly smug about your god-like status, and explode at any mere mortal who dares to forget it.'

'Nope,' he said decisively, grinning. 'I do have a healthy dose of necessary arrogance. Well hidden, of course, beneath my modest and attractively boyish charm. But it's too uncomfortable being a god. . . Too formal and stiff. Like this shirt.' He ran his finger around the inside of the stiff white collar. He looked. . . Well, she was melting at the sight of him in dark pants and a tweedy sports jacket and tie. Something about that conservative, formal clothing only drew her thoughts more strongly to the leonine physicality of the strong body beneath.

'How soon do you think I can get it off, Dr Stone?' he was saying.

'Get what off?'

'This shirt. . .'

'Oh. . .' Taking his meaning and blushing deliciously, she had to say, 'Unless you want me turning up purely to sleep in your bed. . .'

'Sounds perfect!'

'. . .Not till about ten tonight, probably.' She grimaced with resignation. 'Gaye's having a lunch for the Scanner Appeal Committee.'

'You're not on it, are you?'

'No, but I'm a sort of floating volunteer, and I promised. The details of the ball have to be finalised today.'

'Right. . .'

'Have you got your tickets?' She was rather arch.

'Not yet. Can I take *you*, Megan?' Now why was that question, in his deep growl of a voice, so unspeakably arousing?

'Yes, please,' she managed. 'And then tonight I'm going to Carol Bernard's for supper at six. I can't get away *too* early, and I don't want to. She's lonely in Camberton.'

'You're not, I hope.'

'Not any more. . .'

'Ten if you can, then. Better late than not at all.' His need and impatience mirrored her own. 'Meanwhile. . . Is there a linen cupboard handy?'

'A *linen* cupboard?'

'That's the traditional place for illicit dalliance between hospital staff, isn't it? I've just *got* to kiss you before you go. . .'

They found a cleaners' room instead and kissed very thoroughly amongst the mops and floor polishers, then took reluctant leave of each other. Megan went to look for Gary at Peter's bedside but he'd gone home to have lunch and do his midday thumps so she introduced herself to Peter, who was fretting fuzzily, still heavily medicated, at the discomfort of his complicated traction arrangement.

Then she drove to Gaye's, knowing that she was going to be late and certain that the reason for her uncharacteristic lack of punctuality must be written all over her, especially after the most recent kiss. Her mouth still felt swollen and the rest of her was lazy and languorous with awareness and repletion. She was rapidly discovering that there was something utterly delicious about having the sensual secret of a night of love-making in her mind, and wanted to confess it all to Gaye. . .and yet at the same time hug it to herself like some just-discovered treasure.

'It's no good thinking of secrecy,' she said to herself in the car, a vague smile refusing to leave her face, 'because Gaye's going to guess the minute I walk in. . .'

But Gaye was too busy and frazzled to guess anything. '*Why* did I let Derek talk me into going on this committee?' she snarled as soon as she met Megan at the door. 'Mrs Gledhill is *impossible*! She wants hand-carved ice sculptures on every table! I agree it's got to be nice for what we're charging but, good heavens, this is a *fund-raiser* for a provincial hospital, not the society event of the year! We'd have no profit left at all. . . Whereas the florist I've been negotiating with has offered a *very* good deal—'

She broke off abruptly as they reached the dining-room, where a savoury buffet lunch was in progress, and her tone became bright and falsely breezy as she said, 'Do all of you know Dr Stone? Megan, as I'm sure she'd prefer. . .'

The afternoon seemed endless, and Megan's wits were so woolly that she decided Gaye was probably classing her in the same category as the impossible Mrs Gledhill as far as making any useful contribution went. She offered to ring the function centre where the event was being held then forgot what she was supposed to be asking, and when she was given a calculator and told to tot up some numbers she kept pressing the wrong buttons and had to start from the beginning of the long column three times.

'Now, on The Night, we need someone graceful and glamorous to take the seating plan and direct people to their tables,' Mrs Gledhill decreed, for once appropriately. 'Dr Stone. . .?'

'Megan, you *would* be perfect,' Gaye agreed, and all nine committee ladies turned to look at her.

She blushed. Yes, she did feel graceful, very lazily so, after last night and very at ease with her body. But not quite glamorous in the grey wool pants, cream cotton blouse and royal blue angora pullover she'd jumped into at home— between the elephant house and the hospital. She cleared her throat, attempted to dismiss Callum Priestley from pride of place in her thoughts and said, 'Yes, I'd be very happy to do that. There's always a very slight chance I may get called in to the hospital, but if so. . .'

'Then *I'll* do it,' Mrs Gledhill interrupted grandly which, not to overstate the case, rather negated her earlier point about 'graceful and glamorous'.

The meeting ended at last and Megan stayed to help Gaye clear up, certain that *now* the truth would all come out. How could Gaye not see? How could Megan herself avoid a dreamy confession? But Gaye's bustling, impatient movements with the dishes and ceaseless sputtering—at Mrs Gledhill, Mrs Hawthwicke and the preposterous notion of lobster for the first course—didn't exactly create a mood of intimacy.

At half past five Megan left at last, to go straight to Carol's, torn between a gloating pleasure that her passionate secret was still intact and a disappointment that she hadn't been able to relive a little of last night in the telling. Not that she intended to tell too much. . .

Supper at Carol's was pleasant—a chicken casserole with rice, and lots of gossip. Carol admitted with a degree of reticence that she had a date in the wind. 'I don't want to say too much in case I jinx it, superstitious old crone that I am!' And Megan surrendered her own secret enough to say, 'A few weeks ago I'd have been jealous, but now. . .'

'Someone really nice?'

'Oh, I think so. . .' I know so. I've discovered a diamond inside a piece of flinty rock, and I don't know why I've been so lucky. . .

And at twenty past nine she couldn't contain her impatience any longer, put down her empty dessert plate and said, totally failing to sound casual and regretful, 'Must go, I think.'

Carol got a twinkle in her eye. 'Ooh, it *is* going well!'

For the tenth time that day Megan blushed. And in fifteen minutes she would be in Callum's arms. . .

In fact, she spent rather a lot of time in Callum's arms over the next two weeks.

Mainly at his place—they even did some token work on the big house—but in other locations as well. At the cinema, for instance, entwined together in the darkness of the back row like two teenagers so that afterwards Callum said with typical bluntness, 'Well, I don't know why we bothered with a film because I don't have a clue what it was about!' And she certainly couldn't summarise the plot for him.

At restaurants too—holding hands across the table between courses. Kissing, when they dared. And in his office one day where Cecily Stark caught them and had to make a precipitate retreat, distinctly flustered.

'Oh, dear. . .!' Megan said as she straightened her blouse and tenderly blotted her bright lipstick from Callum's face. 'Oh, *dear*. . .!'

'Not to worry,' he growled cheerfully. 'Since I'm almost certain she knows what a slow burn you've had me on for the past millennium she's probably so pleased she'll start knitting you something for Christmas.'

Meanwhile, of course, the demands of the hospital didn't magically switch off. Having to school herself to maintain her usual disciplined focus on the technical demands of her job—correctly reading observations and test result figures, making diagnoses and projecting treatments—Megan found that she was exceptionally well tuned to her patients' emotional states. Too much so, perhaps, as she was in tears of joy or rage about twice a day over a positive prognosis or an interfering relative. Fortunately she always managed to contain herself until she was alone.

Gary Henley was high on her list of priorities. His friend Peter was stable and well now—on full meals, avid about television and fretting at 'being hung up like a trussed chicken', as he phrased it. Gary was astonishingly patient, encouraging and perceptive of Peter's needs...or perhaps it wasn't so astonishing.

'I just think about every fantasy I've ever had of what someone might bring me in hospital, and try to make it happen for Peter,' he said.

'What sort of fantasies?' Megan had to enquire, somewhat suspicious.

He shrugged and grinned. 'Well, I've brought two girls in to see him. *Very* sympathetic, they both were. That traction equipment is impressive! And since he's fancied both of them like mad for the past six months...'

'Oh, Gary...'

'I call it "The Battle of the Nightingales" now. They're both trying to outdo each other in ministering to his every, er, *need.*'

'*Gary*!' She was relieved to remember that Peter's technologically induced immobility would prevent any flagrant and scandalous breaking of certain hospital rules.

Chris Kennedy, of course, was another matter. They were letting Gary in to see him now, at least, but he was still very dependent on modern medical technology. Again, though, Gary's cystic fibrosis became—for the first time in his life—a resource instead of a liability, and he was as tender with his friend as the best-trained nurse. One morning, when Megan and Callum happened to be visiting Chris at the same time, they came across Gary on his way out of the cubicle, looking concerned.

'He wants his pillows moved. I wasn't sure if I should.'

'They can be moved,' Callum said. 'But ask Staff Nurse Jonas. She'd appreciate your help with it, I expect.'

Later, in the corridor on their way out, Callum asked Megan, 'Has he got a job, young Gary?'

'Not at the moment. His CF hasn't permitted, nor any further education. He's had some bad periods over the past couple of years. I'm afraid it's only a matter of time before he's in hospital, waiting for a transplant, although he's bounced back very well lately.'

'But he could hold down something part-time, couldn't he?'

'He's had a couple of things, but he's had to leave. Most employers who will take unskilled young people aren't too sympathetic about heavy, erratic needs for sick leave.'

'Because the hospital's recruiting a new batch of part-time orderlies, I noticed. He'd be good if he was strong enough.'

'And if he wanted to. This hospital isn't exactly his favourite place.'

But she was wrong about that, as it turned out. Callum mentioned the idea to Gary in passing one day and the latter reached Megan on the phone in her office at the first opportunity. 'Do you think I could? I'm stronger than I look. I'm still on my night feeds, and that's really helping. Would you write a reference for me, Dr Stone?'

'I would, yes,' she answered him, 'but I'm surprised you want to, Gary. You always seem to hate it here.' She remembered the real depression that many of his bouts of hospitalisation had caused him, and the time she had put in to help him through it.

'When I'm a patient,' he pointed out. 'Wouldn't you? But coming here to be with Chris and Pete has made me see the place differently. I think I'd have something to offer.'

'You'd certainly have that,' she agreed. But would he have the stamina and strength? Impulsively, after he'd rung off, she got on the phone to Personnel and asked them to send her the job descriptions for any part-time vacancies coming up. Something on Children's, perhaps. . .

'They're going to have him in for an interview,' she told Callum at his place a day or two later. 'I hope we haven't just got his hopes up to have it all end in disappointment. They want an independent medical examination, as well as a report from his CF clinic. They'll hire him if they possibly can, I think, but. . .' She wrung her hands a little.

But Callum was more matter-of-fact. 'Gary's pretty tough, don't you think? It's a disappointment he'd get over. Better than not being given a chance at all.'

'True. If it didn't work out he'd make some joke about not looking good in the uniform. But he's had so many disappointments. Would you believe he wanted to be a jet fighter pilot? Out of the question, of course. I hope this new idea is something he doesn't have to "get over".'

'Come here, you. I didn't lure you to my den to have you worry about your patients all night.'

'Really? Then why *did* you lure me here?' she said archly, impatient for an answer that came in touch, not words.

'If you don't know by now, Dr Stone. . .'

'Tell me. Show me. I'm a slow learner, I'm afraid. . .'

'Really? OK, then. Well, I thought a bit of this might be nice, and then some of this. . .'

There was a familiarity to his touch now that did absolutely nothing to lessen its power and his flagrant and unashamed desire for her, expressed in the feverish wash of his hands across her body and the male need that pulsed and pressed against her hips as he took kiss after kiss from her mouth, only enflamed her own senses even more.

It was six o'clock in the evening and she had come here straight from work, arriving just a few minutes after he did. It was becoming rapidly apparent that, like most of their evenings, this one wasn't going to proceed in the customary order of dinner, civilised entertainment and then bed. She had been hungry on her way here but suddenly that didn't seem to matter at all, and she happily relegated dinner to some time much, much later in the evening. . .

In fact, it was nearly two hours before he slid his warm, hard body reluctantly from hers. 'These early evening naps are very refreshing, aren't they?' was his teasing mutter, and she brazenly propped herself against the pillows with the quilt heaped up to her waist and watched him dress, loving his habit at home of simply dragging a baggy sweatshirt over the bare skin of his torso.

'Come on, lazy!' he told her, hands on his jeaned hips. 'Does this mean *I* have to get dinner?'

'I'm coming, I'm coming.'

'Shall we have that other batch of the stuffed pasta shells we made last week?'

'Well, I'm pretty hungry, yes. . .'

So he disappeared to put it in the microwave as she searched for her far-flung clothing. Picking up her bra, she smiled wickedly as she remembered his cavalier treatment of a similar garment two and a half weeks ago and put it aside again, wearing only black leggings and her soft blue angora pullover on top.

Then she realised that she'd forgotten to take her pill today so she got the packet from her bag on the couch and went into the kitchen for water, not thinking much about the gesture—still too caught up in the languorous afterglow of Callum's breath-taking passion.

He turned just as she reached the sink and saw the foil packet, each pill in its own separate plastic bubble. He didn't need to look twice to know what it was. 'You're on the Pill,' he said, carefully casual, just as she popped it into her mouth.

She nodded. 'Actually, I was having some menstrual problems a few months ago and my GP thought that six months of it might help. It's, um, come in handy now, though, hasn't it?'

'Yes,' he said in a rather stilted way. 'I'm sorry. We didn't even discuss it. I should have asked.'

'That's fine,' she assured him, a little unhappy about his tone. He was frowning, too. She went on, 'I would have said something if we'd needed to. . .discuss precautions.'

'OK. Good. It's settled, then.'

'Yes. Unless. . .'

'No, as long as you're happy with it.'

'Well, I am.'

'Good. Now, er, let's see. . . Do you want salad? Wine? Or mineral water?'

'Mineral water. And salad, yes. No, I'll make it, Callum.'

The meal was on the table within half an hour, and he teased her about the Scanner Appeal ball on the coming Saturday. 'Please be glamorous! You do it so well!' The tone sounded a little forced, but the words distracted her from this fact.

'Oh, I don't!' she insisted. 'I'm a total fraud. Like you, I usually just want to get out of the dress and into some jeans.'

'That makes an attractive picture. . .'

'What, me in jeans?'

'No, you getting out of a dress. Do you have one? Sweeping and long and *décolleté*?'

'Actually, courtesy of cousins in the home counties who keep getting married and having me as a bridesmaid. . .'

'Glamorous cousins, I hope.'

'How does sea-purple velour sound? With a portrait neckline?'

And yet, was it just her imagination or was there something on his mind? After the late meal they sprawled together on the couch and watched television—too tired for anything else—and went to bed at eleven, drifting there on a tide of kisses that threatened to swell and flare all too easily into something much deeper. Lifting the royal blue pullover above her head, she saw that he was watching the sudden spill of her full breasts and loved the green fire of arousal she saw in his eyes.

There was something almost humbling about being able to produce that response in Callum, and something very warm in feeling the same about him. When he came hungrily towards her—unable to wait until they were both fully unclothed—she fell against him then arched to meet his kiss, her nipples grazing the soft cloth of the sweatshirt he still wore.

And when his beeper suddenly sounded on the small table by the bed it seemed like the cruellest interruption.

'I have to go in,' he reported quickly a minute later and she nodded, hugging her arms across her still-naked breasts. He was gone before she could even ask for a kiss.

Slowly she continued to undress, then was suddenly cold. Finding under his pillow the cotton nightshirt he wore—not often, these days—she put it on and loved the feeling of being enveloped in something that went next to his skin, something which smelled deliciously of him and the soap he used. It was some kind of compensation for this sudden loneliness, anyway, but she brooded for some time before sleep came.

He had definitely been holding something back tonight; he had been absorbed in thoughts he wasn't sharing with her. Thoughts that concerned her, though, she was sure of it.

When he returned she had only just plunged into a deep, fatigued sleep, and was groggy and disorientated as he slipped in beside her. 'What was it?' she managed.

'Congenital heart defect on a newborn,' he said. 'He'll live. . .now. Don't talk. It's after one.' He reached across and touched her briefly, then laughed. 'You're wearing my nightshirt.'

'I was cold.'

'Go to sleep. . .' And he rolled away from her. Minutes later she slipped into oblivion and was not to know how long Callum himself lay stiffly, staring into the darkness— his mind churning with issues of confidence and doubt, right and wrong, gallantry and selfish need. . .

Next morning they were up at half past six, with little time for sensuality or snuggling.

'I'll shower, you eat. Then vice versa,' he decreed, and they were both ready to leave the house half an hour later.

The fact that he hadn't talked over breakfast, Megan thought, and the fact that he didn't stop to kiss her before they left the warmth of his small house. . .didn't it just mean that they were both in a hurry to get to work on time?

But then, when she already had her car keys in hand and they were about to separate and take different routes through the winter-bare mess of garden, 'Are you coming again tonight, Megan?'

'If. . . If you. . .' Oh, why prevaricate? Why pretend? '*Yes!*'

Then he spoke the words which anyone would have agreed were ominous in a relationship, 'Because we need to talk.' He had turned away from her already, and she couldn't see his eyes.

CHAPTER NINE

IT WAS a long day. Megan began with rounds, joining Tony Glover and several others on the men's side of the chest ward as soon as she arrived. There had been several new admissions since yesterday and, consequently, some thorny problems to discuss. Hopefully, at least, the teaching session which resulted would be useful for the medical students in attendance. Later there were office appointments and a clinic, more patients to see on the ward and, finally, test results to study and case notes to write up.

With the sense that there were still things on her desk left undone, she left the hospital at seven—almost twelve hours since she had arrived. It had been dark then and it was dark now, and the thought of seeing Callum—he'd been hoping to get away fairly early today, and had 'almost promised' he'd be there by six—was exceptionally sweet. Except for that parting phrase of his this morning, which had been drumming in her mind during walks between wards and office, cafeteria and clinic all day.

Talk? They could talk tonight. . .now. . .for as long as he liked—about whatever he wanted—as long as he was holding her and smiling at her. But what if he wasn't? What if he wanted to say that this whole intoxicating thing between them had been a mistake? It did happen. He said he'd been in love with her for four years, but perhaps it had been better in fantasy than reality. Some people. . . some men. . .were like that, weren't they? The glory was all in the chase. And of late she hadn't given him any chasing to do at all.

Her stomach was wound into a tight little ball when she arrived at his place, parking at the front and walking quickly through the untamed yard, past the monstrosity of a house that—sharing Callum's vision now—she knew would one day look so good. Beyond the straggle of hedge his own little dwelling was lit by a welcoming yellow glow from within, and her ringing steps on the broken cement path quickened.

In two minutes I'll be in his arms and I'll know that I've been an idiot to worry today.

Because, at some level, her faith in the intensity of what she felt made a mockery of her fears.

She knocked at the big wooden door, thinking, Any day he's going to suggest getting my own key. . . I want to be here with him every spare moment! He opened it seconds later, holding it defensively just a little ajar and shielding her view of the cosy interior with his big body.

'Hi,' she managed, her palm suddenly damp.

'Could you not stay tonight after all, Megan?' he began decisively at once. 'I tried to ring you at the hospital a few minutes ago, but obviously—'

'What's wrong?' she demanded. 'Of course I won't stay if you're—'

'I'm sorry.' He had a shuttered look on his ruggedly drawn features. 'Something's come up. Something. . . really unexpected. I can't see you for a few days, that's all.'

'OK, but—'

'I can't talk now. I'll pick you up on Saturday for the Scanner Appeal thing, as arranged.'

'You've got me worried, Callum,' she blurted out.

He was still blocking the doorway and there were other people inside, she was sure of it. She heard a female voice coming from the kitchen.

'Yes, I know,' he said. 'I—Things have changed a bit. Give me some time, all right?'

'Time?' she echoed. 'OK. . .' What else could she say? He had already closed the door and disappeared and she fled, the threat of tears burning behind her eyes and in her throat.

Saturday. She had to wait until Saturday, and it was only Wednesday now. Thursday and Friday crawled by.

'Listen to my great big deep breathing!' Bhasa Singh said during a follow-up appointment in the chest department's examining rooms on Thursday afternoon. Her dark little face was alive with pride and she heaved her shoulders up and down and puffed her chest out like a pouter pigeon.

But, six-year-old exaggeration aside, her breathing *was* good.

Mrs Singh was very happy. 'We saw Mr Priestley and Dr Baxter on Tuesday, and they say her heart is in perfect shape now. She's putting on weight, don't you think, Dr Stone?'

'She certainly looks much, much better.'

'She's doing well at school, and she's so good with Prakash, aren't you, love?'

'I can change him and sing to him. He loves me!'

'Of course he does, Bhasa,' Megan said with a smile. What smug certainty! 'I bet you're a terrific sister!'

But after they'd gone—along with a procession of patients with emphysema and chronic bronchitis and asthma, all of whom needed her encouragement, praise, concern and concentration—well, it was hard to keep up a front and, back in her office on the first floor, she slumped a little at the thought of notes to write up and a late-afternoon check to make on her hospital patients.

A cup of tea? The panacea offered in hospitals and doctors' rooms across the country—out of all proportion to its actual abilities as a healing or soothing agent. . . But right now it would be nice. She left her small office and went along to the kitchen—to find that her Earl Grey tea had disappeared again. So much for buying an expensive brand as a treat to enjoy! Resolving to keep it in her desk from now on, she went up to the second floor to hunt for it and—as if life had gone into action replay—there was Cecily Stark, fiddling with the coffee machine.

'I'm looking for my—'

'I just saw it next to the biscuits on the top shelf,' Mrs Stark said drily, and Megan rolled her eyes.

'Thanks!'

'I. . .er. . .if I find out who it is that's taking it, I'll give them a ticking off on your behalf, shall I?' This was accompanied by further proof that Cecily Stark *could* smile after all.

'Don't worry,' Megan said. 'I'm going to keep it locked away from now on. Um, coffee for Callum?' She gestured at the electric percolator.

'Yes. He's in. Do you need to see him?'

'No, no. I expect he's very busy. Our. . .schedules aren't coinciding for the next couple of days.'

She fielded a shrewd glance from Callum's secretary by the simple expedient of looking down at her fingernails to minutely scrutinise a non-existent tear.

'He *is* busy,' the older woman said. She added, after a small hesitation, 'He has family members visiting him at the moment.'

'I see. . .' Megan nodded, aware of Mrs Stark's ongoing examination. He hadn't mentioned it. But, of course. . . why should he?

'Having family isn't always easy.' Mrs Stark seemed to be choosing her words carefully. 'I'm expecting him not to be quite *himself* while they're here. I'm going to make allowances.'

The hint was so careful and yet so pointed that Megan couldn't help saying, 'And that's what I should do too?'

'I think so, dear. . . I think it would be the sensible thing.'

'Thank you, for—'

'Mr Priestley is a very special kind of man,' came the

cryptic interruption. 'That doesn't mean he comes maintenance-free, with a full set of instructions.'

Since Megan didn't know what to say to this at all it was perhaps fortunate that Mrs Stark set her percolator going at that point and then promptly disappeared.

Returning to make the tea in the kitchen on the floor below, Megan considered the exchange. That it was meant to be reassuring, she had no doubt. But is it this obvious that I'm miserable about him? she fretted.

Perhaps only to someone like Cecily Stark, who seemed to watch her employer's emotional state like a hawk.

She couldn't know, though, Megan decided. If he's having doubts, she wouldn't know. And what 'family members' does he have visiting? Why hasn't he told me?

The painfully slow ticking away of Friday's hours was punctuated by several phone calls—the first from Gary Henley.

'I've got it!' he reported triumphantly. 'Just heard! I had the interview and medical exam yesterday, and Julie Stebbins at my clinic must have put in a good word. I'm to start in ten days. Just Saturday and Sunday from seven until three, and one or two rotating evenings during the week from three until nine, in the children's wing. . .' He told her every detail and she was thrilled for him.

'We'll meet up there, then, now that we're colleagues,' she told him, and typically his reply was blunt and honest.

'Colleagues? Don't make me laugh! Opposite ends of the pecking order, and don't I know it! It won't be, ''How are you, Gary?'' any more, it'll be, ''Orderly, why isn't this patient down in Radiology? She should have been there half an hour ago!'' '

'Well, you'll just have to make sure you're *not* late, then, won't you?' she retorted cheerfully.

'See what I mean? No sympathy from the doctors! What if the lift was stuck? What if Sister was behind with the blood drawing?'

'Gary, you're going to be very good at this job. You know all the excuses already, and you haven't even started yet.'

'In three weeks I'll have my first pay cheque. Meanwhile, Chris is almost ready to start on the same social programme I'm running for Pete. . .'

'Oh, *no*!'

'Eh?' He was indignant in the extreme. 'Vital form of recreational therapy, Dr Stone!'

He rang off, still exultant, and she had to giggle for a moment. Encountering Gary trundling small patients around the hospital was going to be a lift to anyone's spirits.

If only the effect lasted which, in her case today, it didn't. More hours plodded by—seeing three patients, conferring with radiology about some X-rays and politely blasting a lazy GP over a screamingly obvious diagnosis of moderately severe cystic fibrosis which the man had missed. Then her beeper sounded rather unexpectedly after a lengthy emergency down in Casualty, and it was Gaye Wyman trying to reach her.

'I've been ringing your office on and off all day,' she complained.

'Yes, I've been all over the place. What's up?'

'Well, I know I said I wouldn't need you until tomorrow night, but. . .'

'Of course I can come in earlier, Gaye,' she soothed.

'Rose Paxton is sick and Cynthia Gledhill, *of course*, has a two-hour hair appointment right in the middle of the afternoon, just when we need her.'

'So, when do you want me, exactly?'

'Um, from one until six? If you have other plans. . .'

'No. . . I don't.' But I wish I did!

And when she heard Callum's voice on the phone back in her office later on she hoped, of course, that he was going to suggest something for tomorrow after all. It was a little shaming to realise that she would have been almost as impossible as Mrs Gledhill with her hair if it had come to the point.

Perhaps it was fortunate, then. . .*perhaps* it was. . .that he wasn't making a personal call at all.

'Look, I'd like another opinion on Chris Kennedy's lungs, Megan. Can you come and look at him this afternoon?'

'Of course,' she told him. 'I'm just winding up here for the week. It can wait. I can come now, if you'd like.'

'Yes, that'd fit in well. Can I meet you at his bedside in five minutes, then?'

Chris was out of Intensive Care now, but still not yet ready to go home.

'We can't get rid of these pulmonary infections,' Callum told her when they met outside the ward. 'It's setting him back and we keep having to re-intubate.'

'I bet Jim Allyson is beside himself.'

'He is! So am I, a bit! We've done sputum cultures and this antibiotic ought to be getting rid of the bug, but it isn't. Am I missing something?'

His look was an appeal, and she thought, He didn't need to have me come to the bedside for this. He could have said it over the phone. Doesn't that mean he wants to see me? Aloud she said, 'Nothing obvious. But I can solve the problem, all the same.'

'What would I do without you. . .?' was his light response.

Wither away, I hope, like I would! But he hadn't meant it that way. It was just a throw-away line because Jim Allyson had prowled over from the nurses' station, and was listening somewhat suspiciously.

Gathering her thoughts, she told him, 'There's been a study done recently that shows the antibiotic you've been using works far better *in vitro* than it does in the lung itself. For some reason it doesn't penetrate the lung tissue

well enough, but there's something new available now.'
She named a recently developed drug of the penicillin
family. 'It's said to work much better.'

'Let's see if they're right, then,' Callum nodded.

Then Jim Allyson cut in, still suspicious, 'Do you have
the details on those studies, Dr Stone?'

'I can get them for you if you'll ring my office on
Monday.'

'I will!' He nodded decisively, and made a note in his
small diary.

'Thanks for that,' Callum said as they left the surgical
ward. 'Walking back to the other building now?'

'Yes, actually.' So they fell into step together and left
the main building in silence.

So far they had been very discreet around the hospital
about their blossoming new relationship, and she had
decided thankfully on more than one occasion over the
past few weeks that no one suspected. There had been
something cosy and special about the secrecy, since it
wasn't hurting anyone, and the wickedly covert looks and
touches she had received from Callum were things she
had gloated over and hugged to herself.

Now he didn't touch her at all, openly or otherwise,
and she saw that secrecy had another more bitter benefit—
you saved your pride if the thing ended.

Was it ending? Had it already? Megan wasn't the kind
of person to let it go without a fight.

'I ran into Mrs Stark today,' she said abruptly. 'She
told me you had family visiting.'

He threw her an unreadable look. 'Yes, my dad and. . .
my stepmother. I wasn't expecting them, actually.'

'No, I gathered not since you'd made no mention of
them.' She knew how stiff she sounded.

'I'm sorry, Megan. . .'

'What for?'

'For—Oh hell, we can't talk about it now.'

'We can. I want to, Callum. I—'

'No.' His shoulders were hunched and his hands thrust
deep into the pockets of his dark trousers. The cold grey
wind that hit them as they crossed the car park to the
medical building gave his black hair a rough combing. 'I
don't even know yet what I've got to say,' he went on
bluntly. 'Give me some time, OK?'

'Sure. Sure.' It was the same thing he'd said the other
day. She volunteered miserably, 'If the ball tomorrow is
awkward. . .'

'No, no. They're going tomorrow morning. They're on
their honeymoon, actually.'

'Honeymoon? So you're feeling a bit like a novice
Cinderella?'

His laughter was a rough bark. 'Cinderella? I expect
that's part of the problem, yeah!'

So I can still make him laugh at least. . .

They separated moments later and she got through the
rest of the afternoon then saw him again as she left the
medical office building at six, standing just yards away,
outside the nondescript entrance. He was with an older
man who, although shorter and fatter, looked so much like
him that their relationship was completely apparent and a
female who, at first glance and from the back, could have
been in her early twenties.

A closer view from the front, though—as she drove past
them in her car on her way out—showed a blowsy-looking
woman of at least forty-five, with brittle, over-bleached
hair, weather-beaten skin beneath too-heavy make-up and
clothing that would have been brassy on a twenty-two-
year-old model. Slowing to negotiate the speed bumps in
front of the main entrance Megan caught Callum's eye
for a fraction of a second as he ushered his father and
stepmother inside.

'They must have asked for a tour,' she said to herself. 'I
expect his dad is painfully proud of him. . . That's lovely!'

But Callum didn't look as if he was enjoying the exercise very much at all.

'You've checked all the table settings, Megan?' Gaye demanded late on Saturday afternoon.

'Yes, all in order. The flowers are beautiful.'

'All the place-cards and menus are in place?'

'Yes.'

'No one's missing any cutlery?'

'No.'

'Now, there was something else... Oh, heavens! The banner! Look, you and I will have to do that together. Muriel and Barbara are sweet and helpful but not very athletic. Much better to keep them setting out donation envelopes and arranging flowers for the dais. Gosh, is it nearly five already?'

'Five past, actually.'

Gaye, uncharacteristically, swore. 'Help me in the kitchen, then. I haven't finished the inventory we're supposed to do of the china and glass. We have to cover breakages, you see. I'm beginning to wish we'd picked the place that would have catered it all for us. They were nearly twice the price, but bringing caterers in has turned out to be a lot more trouble than—Anyway, where was I up to? Are there thirty-six cocktail glasses in this box, no chips or cracks?'

They counted and ticked off items on a list for several minutes, then had to climb up on a precarious arrangement of boxes and chairs to lace a huge banner reading CAMBERTON HOSPITAL MRI SCANNER APPEAL to a convenient beam above the dais, which was still alarmingly bare of any musicians' equipment.

'I did phone the band,' Gaye said. 'Twice! They *promised* they were coming!'

'They're professionals, aren't they?' Megan soothed.

'Of course they're coming, and they probably don't take long to set up.'

'You think so?' Gaye said doubtfully.

'Stop *worrying*! The place looks splendiferous and I've just seen two caterers' vans pull up out the front.'

'The *front*? They're supposed to come to the back!' Gaye wailed, leaping dangerously down from her chair. But the vans were already moving again, as the drivers realised their mistake. 'Can you believe this thing starts in two hours?'

'And we're almost finished.'

'Nick and Helen Darnell came to dinner last night,' Gaye said. 'She asked me if I was on a diet! I told her it was purely the pressure of this event.'

'Well, it's an ill wind, then, isn't it?' Megan suggested slyly.

'No, because I'll put it all back on again tonight,' Gaye replied gloomily. 'Black Forest Torte for dessert. And Derek will give me his.'

'You'll be *far* too nervous to eat, Gaye!'

And she had to laugh at the eager brightening of the older woman's face. 'Of course I will! How marvellous!'

'Speaking of the Darnells, though, how are they?' Megan asked, dispassionately aware that she could say that once-hallowed name without the slightest discomfort now. How good *that* felt!

'Oh, super!' Gaye said as she climbed back on to the dais to tie off the ends of the banner. 'The baby is heavenly, and what's even more heavenly for them, I expect, is that Jane is up for the weekend and is going to babysit tonight.'

'How long are they staying?'

'Just a week here and a week or so in London. They fly out again on Boxing Day. They've rented self-catering flats. They've just seen all the autumn colour in New England, they look healthy and happy as anything and—'

She broke off suddenly. 'You're not. . .having trouble with this, are you, Megan?'

'Not in the least.' She met Gaye's searching stare with an easy smile. 'I'm really not, Gaye.'

'No, I can see that.'

Her tone was speculative and she watched Megan for a minute more—saying nothing—then turned away to make a last knot in the banner's cord lacing, which was now threaded through all the eyelets at the back of the expertly painted canvas. Megan held it in position for her, unaware that certain wheels were still turning in Gaye's mind, until she said, 'I haven't even asked, Megan. Who are you bringing tonight?'

'Well, actually,' she prevaricated, 'I wouldn't say that I was bringing anyone. . .'

'Oh. . . Really?' Gaye sounded very disappointed.

Then she had to bite the bullet. 'But Callum Priestley's bringing me.'

Three days ago she wouldn't have been able to keep a creamy smile from her lips. Today she knew she was frowning as she said it, and added quickly before Gaye could comment, 'Don't read anything into it, please. It. . . it just seemed convenient, that's all.'

'*Convenient*? Would Callum really—?'

'He wanted to go. To support the appeal, of course. The hospital needs an MRI scanner. I'm not sure. . .if he's much of a dancer. And he knew I was helping to organise it. So. . .'

'I see,' Gaye nodded, and Megan was immediately aware that she saw all too clearly. 'You're miserably in love with him, aren't you?' the older woman said quietly.

'Yes, *miserably*! A few days ago it was ''blissfully'' and I was dying to tell you, only something suddenly went wrong but I don't know what. And if he's only taking me to this ball out of a sense of honour, because he'd already promised, I'll feel like the little mermaid—Andersen, not Disney—dancing on knives.'

'You don't have any idea?'

'No. He says he "wants to talk",' she drawled, hooking her index fingers around the phrase. 'And isn't *that* a doom-laden expression?'

'Oh, Megan, I'm sure it isn't as black as—' She broke off. 'Yes, Muriel?'

'It's five to six.' The oldest member of the committee craned her neck to look up at them from below the dais. 'I must get home to change. And Harry can't get himself presentable in a dinner suit without my help.'

'Of course. We must all go,' Gaye announced decisively. 'There's really nothing else to do and we should all *try* to be back by a quarter to eight at the latest if we can possibly manage it!'

CHAPTER TEN

MEGAN didn't manage to be back by a quarter to eight. Callum was picking her up at twenty to, and somehow she couldn't face ringing him to suggest such an insignificant change of plan. In any case, showering, drying and styling her hair, and putting on make-up and clothes left her with little time to spare.

So it was almost eight when she arrived at the glittering event, and she had to plunge immediately into her assigned role of directing people to the tables which had been set in a wide U-shape around the extensive dance-floor and on the balcony above.

She and Callum hadn't talked much in the car—just obvious, superficial things. Had his father's and step-mother's visit been a success? He thought so. Were the preparations of the ball in hand? Well, possibly Gaye was too nervous to think so, but everyone else did. Megan looked stunning. Callum looked perfect. Or so they each told the other in a constricted, perfunctory sort of way.

But Callum *did* look perfect. His formal black dinner suit, which fitted without a wrinkle across his broad shoulders or a gape across his equally broad chest, gave a deceptive veneer of civilisation to the untameable body beneath. As relentlessly aware of him as she was, Megan felt that the suit emphasised his maleness—rather than containing or concealing it—and as usual she found that she was helplessly—and, tonight, painfully—aroused by her sense of the contrasts between them.

The sea-purple velour draped and clung to her body, as sensuous and soft as his caress, and the French pleat in her silver-blonde hair left her neck bare and

175

hungry for the warmth of his breath and his lips.

He was clearly preoccupied, and it lent a brooding quality to his face and his stance which would have been very
threatening if she had ever had any inkling that Callum
was capable of easy violence. He wasn't, though, and it
was one of the countless things she now knew that she
loved about him—that all his virility and strength was
expressed in the razor-sharp control of surgery or in his
wrestling with a huge old house.

When they arrived she took the seating plan that Gaye
thrust into her hands and found their own table, where
Callum went to sit at once. Immediately she was besieged
by people—some polite, some impatient—and had to
exercise all her grace, tact and organisational skills to get
them pointed in the direction of the correct table.

Only occasionally over the next half-hour did she get a
change to glance at Callum and she saw that he was flung
untidily into his seat, alone at the table for ten and with
a forbidding expression which discouraged the kind of
mingling that other people were doing.

Yes, there was Derek moving towards him, hesitating
and veering away again to greet Camberton's mayor, Letty
Davis, and her husband, Donald. Nina and Richard
Hartman caught sight of him, too, while Megan was showing them their table, and the latter said to his wife, 'Let's
go over to Callum, shall we, before we take our seats? He
looks lonely. Has he been stood up?'

'No,' said Nina. 'I know that look. He must have had
a difficult day in surgery.'

Turning to the next group, now that the Hartmans were
safely headed for the right table, Megan thought, He probably did, too. That expression's got nothing to do with me
at all. Then she said aloud, 'Table twenty-six? Yes, third
from the end on the left. By the pillar, can you see?'

She lifted her purple-clad arm, then quickly and gracefully held up the floor-length folds of her dress as one of

the table twenty-six people threatened to catch it on her spiked heel as she moved forward. Megan realised that Callum was watching her, but as soon as he caught her eye he stared away again.

His table was still empty and remained so until almost half past eight, when the four other couples designated to sit there arrived within three minutes of each other.

'Mrs Gledhill did the seating,' Gaye had explained a week ago, 'but I told her to put you at a table of people who don't know each other. You don't mind, do you? You can do a bit of introducing; get conversation going.'

'That's fine.'

Only now it wasn't so fine because, having finished her work as usher, all she wanted to do was talk to Callum. Who were these people?

She recognised a woman who was new in Admin, together with her husband, and an elderly couple—the Crandalls—who worked tirelessly as volunteers in the hospital library. There was another couple whom she didn't know at all, and then Karen Graham. . .no, it was Shadwell now. . .who'd been a very competent sister on the men's chest ward, before leaving a couple of years ago to plunge into a disastrous relationship with a former patient.

She had turned up some months later at Linwood Gardens, the nearby day hospital and respite care centre which was under the auspices of Camberton Hospital, and then a far happier romance had blossomed with the man now at her side—Lee Shadwell, himself the exceptionally able nursing manager at Linwood.

'How are you, Karen?' she asked the plumply pretty blonde, who was seated on Callum's left.

But Karen didn't reply. She was, in fact, chewing very desperately on a dry biscuit, and Lee Shadwell came in with easy humour, 'She's deep in the wilds of the first trimester, I'm afraid. Aren't you, my poor love? You'll

be eating cracker biscuits all night, and I'll have to eat
both our meals—since we've paid for them!'

'Sorry,' Karen said to Megan. 'It's wretched. I've had
to take—' She broke off and chewed madly again, waving
her hands in apology.

'Two weeks off work,' Lee finished for her. 'I've been
told to consider our options for sterilisation as we're definitely not doing this again!'

'No! That was yesterday. Bad day! Better now,'
Karen said.

This last assertion, though, wasn't very convincing as
she then immediately got up from the table and plunged
towards the nearest exit. Lee's lithe frame could be seen
moments later, weaving between the late arrivals as he
tried to catch up, bringing two napkins, a pitcher of water
and her packet of biscuits with him.

At least this simplified introductions. Megan performed
the task gracefully, then muttered a drawling 'Thanks!' to
Callum under her breath as he started talking to the
Crandalls in his unpretentious way, rapidly disposing of
their initial flustered awe at being seated with a consultant
cardiothoracic surgeon.

Two courses came and went, as did poor Karen and
Lee—twice—and then there was dancing. It was a glittering affair, with almost all the men in dinner suits and
the women in trailing gowns or deceptively simple little
sheaths. The eight-piece band was said to be versatile and
should include a tempo and mood for everyone, Gaye had
promised.

The Crandalls got to their feet eagerly as soon as the
music began, while the woman from Admin and her husband shook their heads. 'We don't.'

Callum looked at Megan. 'What about us?' he asked
gruffly. 'Do we?'

'I—I'd like to.' I'd like to know for certain that there
is a 'we'.

He rose and she followed him out to the rapidly filling dance-floor, just as a fifties rock and roll number ended and a slow love ballad began.

'That's lucky,' he said drily. 'I was mentally reviewing the procedure for spinning you out to the end of my arm, and I think I'd need a refresher course.'

Reaching out, he took her in his arms—holding her low in the small of her back so that she could feel the heavy warmth of his hands through the slippery velour fabric. Feeling the brush of her forehead against his neck, she longed to turn her face upwards to kiss him there but she didn't dare tonight when she was still so unsure of him. They had both acted as hosts during the first two courses, helping to create a single conversational focus that flowed back and forth across the table. There had been no opportunity for anything private at all.

Would he be doing this if he didn't care? she asked herself, but couldn't answer the question with confidence.

Her own feelings were in too much turmoil for her to be able to read his clearly. Around them on the dance-floor there were familiar faces everywhere. The Wymans, the Hartmans, Rob Baxter and Ariadne Demopoulos—who were an acknowledged couple now—members of the hospital board and their partners, Mrs Gledhill and the small gentleman who must be her better half.

And Nick and Helen Darnell. The music stopped just as they swung past and so all the couples came to a standstill, clapping politely and waiting for the band to launch into another number. The Darnells both caught sight of Megan at the same time and she was suddenly plunged into memories of those awful months two years ago, before they had left for Boston, when she still had to see Nick at work virtually every day and remember what an unforgivable fool she'd made of herself.

She had done everything she could to avoid meeting Helen during that horrible time, wondering if the other woman could ever look on her without enmity—no matter what she managed to do with her own feelings.

But two years had gone by now. Nick had a little more grey in his hair, and Helen was a little fuller around the hips. Her husband clearly didn't mind this latter change. His hand rested there with loving possession until Helen detached herself. She was coming over.

'Megan! How are you?' she said, as the music began again, pressing the slim hand she had seized between her own two slightly warmer ones.

'Oh. . . Very well! And obviously *you* are. . . Congratulations on baby Therese!'

'I'm almost sorry we didn't bring her tonight,' Helen said, her face quite dewy with maternal pride. 'So many people have asked.'

'Did you bring a photo?'

'Not even that. Silly, weren't we?'

Behind her Megan was aware of Callum's shielding presence as he nodded a greeting to Nick, and to Helen as well, then his arm came around her and she realised with a blaze of warmth, He wants them to know we're together. That has to be good. . .

'Nice to see you again too, Callum,' Helen said, and they exchanged news for a minute or two after the music had begun again, then Nick came in with the dry humour that was typical of him.

'We've committed ourselves to the third year in Boston, Megan, so you lot have a fair bit of time to get the chest department back in order again. If you're lucky, I'll never be able to prove that it went to the dogs during my absence.'

'Isn't he awful?' Helen laughed.

'Awful!' Megan agreed, then suddenly, impulsively, she leaned forward and kissed the other woman quickly on the cheek and whispered, 'Thank you for. . . For not. . .' She dried up but Helen kissed her back, understanding

Megan's meaning. Clearly she was sure enough of her husband's love now that she could be generous and forgiving.

'Everyone makes mistakes in love,' she said. 'Isn't it all working out for you now?' She meant Callum, of course.

'I don't know,' Megan managed. 'I honestly don't know.'

'Then find out,' Helen ordered. 'This one *is* meant for you, I think. Gaye's always thought so. Don't let him slip through your fingers.'

'Give me some hints!'

'Don't jump to conclusions. Believe in yourself. He's here now, isn't he? He's holding you. . . He's a magnificent man, Megan.'

'I know *that*. Too well for my own good!'

'I warn you, then, I'll be expecting an update from Gaye once we're back in Boston.'

'That's enough of the girlish secrets, you two,' Nick came in. 'We're creating a bottleneck.'

'Oops. . . Maybe we'll meet up later in the evening,' Helen said.

Another couple swung between them and Callum turned Megan into his strong arms again, saying nothing as they swayed to the music until minutes later, 'Sorry I'm not much of a dance partner. . .'

Since she'd just been thinking how gracefully they moved together, and how it didn't matter at all that no recognised dance steps were being performed, she couldn't help blurting with tender honesty, 'I think you're the most wonderful dance partner I've ever had.'

The music stopped again and he pulled away and looked at her. . . No, *studied* her with grim focus—that stark, almost fierce expression on his face. 'You're. . . incredible.'

'Why?'

'Because you really seem prepared to take me on, lock, stock and barrel.'

'Callum, what are you talking about?'

'My background—which didn't include any ballroom dancing lessons, my tell-tale accent, my masochistic taste in weekend entertainment. . .'

'My God, those aren't things to "take on"!' She searched that face of his, loving every inch of it and wanting to read it to its very depths. She saw the opalescent fire of arousal in his green eyes, then saw it damped and hooded by the sweep of his tired, black-lashed lids. 'What *is* it, Callum?' she pleaded. 'You said you wanted to talk, and I'm. . .well, I'm suffering pretty badly, not knowing what you want to say.'

'Suffering? You don't know what it means!'

'Oh, *don't* I?'

They glared at each other.

'No, you don't,' he growled. '*I'm* suffering. Finding out purely by chance the other day that you were on the Pill and realising how much I'd secretly been hoping. . . assuming. . .that you weren't, and that already I might have managed to start our child growing inside you. It made me hungry for you, just thinking about it, and it made me realise how much I *wanted* something like that to bind us together against all odds.'

'Wh—? Odds. . .? Callum—'

'Which was a pretty wonderful and pretty terrifying shock in itself to know I felt that deeply about you. I've had to work too hard until recently to think about marriage. . . And my first girlfriend at university was somewhat scathing about the likelihood of anyone ever wanting to dip into my questionable gene pool to generate some offspring. . . And then to discover that it was impossible; that there couldn't be a baby because you were on the Pill, which probably meant that you had doubts about my gene pool, too—'

'Callum, I told you why I was on the—'

'I know,' he growled. 'I'm not saying this all makes sense, you know. But the fact is, despite certain elements of irrationality in my thinking, I was suddenly slammed with the very rational realisation that I didn't have the right to ask for it all with you as I wanted—God, as I want—to do.'

'Don't have the *right*?'

'Come on, Megan, don't deny that there's a difference between our backgrounds. My God, when Dad turned up the other day with Imogene in tow. . .! The timing couldn't have been worse. Realising I wanted to marry you—make children together, bind our lives utterly—then suddenly being presented with a nightmare of a stepmother, who I couldn't even imagine in the same room with you.'

'Is she so totally terrible? She looked—'

'No, no, she's not totally terrible,' he conceded impatiently. 'She's quite sweet underneath. She means well. But she's everything that you're not. Cheap and tarty and pretentious and. . .rather crude. I heard much more about Dad's sex life with her than I wanted to. And she drinks. Along with Dad. Till they both get loud and sozzled and cruder than ever.

'When you came to my place on Wednesday evening and they were there I just couldn't face having to introduce you and listen to the awful, stilted conversation I knew would follow. Them turning up like that just seemed to be a message from a fairly malicious providence saying, "There! What on earth gives you the right to expect it of her?"

'I had to think that there was another not strictly medical reason for the Pill; that this was just some temporary kick for you, safe from any murky consequences that might doom you to a permanent association.'

'Temporary. . .? Murky consequences?' Having listened to him in stunned disbelief, followed by a groping understanding, she was almost shaking with anger now. 'Murky, Callum? Being mother to your child?' They were both utterly oblivious of the music and the dancers as they stood together, length pressed to length but with their eyes spitting sparks at each other.

'Do you really think I'd have risked making a fool of myself a *second* time? That I'd have tried so hard to get us both over what happened two years ago out of some shallow—' She couldn't finish. 'And that the existence of a dubious father and stepmother would be enough to— I'm insulted that you could think that of me! You've really insulted me, Callum Priestley!'

Angry tears pricked in her eyes and she blinked them furiously away. 'Not to mention giving me four days of horrible doubt on top of the needless two years I'd already put myself through!'

She whirled away from him and fled through the crowd of dancers, swept by a morass of feelings she couldn't sort out at all. A moment later she tripped over her own dress and felt it tear beneath the heel of her shoe, then gasped as Callum's arms caught her up and spun her roughly back to him in his haste to save her from falling. The portrait neckline of the purple gown pulled low on her shoulders and across her breasts, which heaved with the pull of her quickened breathing.

'Could you be right?' he whispered harshly. 'My God, I think you are!'

She seized on his doubts furiously, and his intensity banished her own. 'Of course I am! I love you, Callum. You've heard me say it enough, haven't you? I didn't add "for now" or "quite a bit, considering your background" or "but I wouldn't want your children". I just meant "I love you" and I meant everything about you, and I need you to. . .I *thought* you felt the same.'

'I did. Bloody hell, I do! Oh, Megan, can't you tell how much?'

'How much?' she whispered.

'Enough to make me doubt everything I've always been sure about—which is that I'm proud of who I am and where I came from, what I've made of my life and that I don't need to apologise for any of it. Not my mum pickling herself or my crummy vowels, or. . .'

'Or your dad, or Imogene, or being *hungry* until you were eight years old! You *should* be proud of it all, Callum. I am. . .'

'Enough to marry me, Megan?'

'Just try suggesting anything else! I've thought since Wednesday that you wanted to end it. . .'

'I did. For your sake. I was doing the noble thing, renouncing my heart. For the sake of—'

'My genes?' she suggested tartly. 'Since I'm the off-spring of highly desirable upper-crust drunks, instead of nasty working-class ones? That makes all the difference!'

But he completely ignored her sarcasm and whispered, 'It turns out I'm not noble enough, though, because I know now that I'm not ending this as long as I live.' His arms slid around her still more strongly as he buried his face in her neck and left a trail of fire with his lips. She arched and gasped at his touch, then they both remembered where they were and drew away a little, laughing.

'You'll have to introduce me to that cousin of yours,' he said slyly.

'Which one?'

'The one who put her bridesmaids in this stunning dress. If I nudged it and nuzzled it a little bit more, would it slip all the way down?'

'Callum. . .'

'What are you wearing underneath?'

'*Callum*!'

'You're right—whatever it is I can't do justice to its removal here in public. Could we possibly leave?'

'No, we couldn't possibly leave,' she told him firmly. . .

and regretfully. 'I'm supposed to be announcing the amount we've raised so far during the speeches after dessert. Gaye would never forgive me.'

'She's coming towards us now, as it happens.'

The poor woman still looked flustered, in her pale green gown, as if she had the cares of the entire National Health Service resting on her solitary shoulders.

'Oh, dear,' Megan murmured. 'I hope this isn't a problem with dessert.'

But Gaye had a far trickier issue on her mind. 'Have you two finished yet?' she demanded distractedly.

'Finished?' They both echoed, bemused.

'Yes. Finished. Your fight. Sorted things out. I've been wanting to ask the band to wind down this set for the past ten minutes so we can get on with the dessert course, but you obviously hadn't finished making up so I've held off. Can I do it now?'

'Yes, Gaye, do it now,' Callum growled.

'Oh, good! Thanks!' she said vaguely, and wandered off in the direction of the dais. Seconds later they heard faintly, flung back over her shoulder, 'Congratulations, by the way. But I'm not offering to organise the wedding!'

'Actually, I think we'd like to organise that ourselves, wouldn't we?' Callum murmured to Megan, quite unperturbed by the curious and amused glances from the people—quite a number of them—who had overheard Gaye's last defiant words.

'Mmm, I think so.' She turned into his arms again to dance, wishing that they *hadn't* told Gaye that she could order an end to the slow, romantic song.

'We've got a lot to do, then, haven't we?' he murmured.

'Yes, the wedding, the Callum J. Priestley Home for—'

'—Terminally Love-struck Surgeons.'

'And that baby we've agreed on, despite the mutually questionable genes. . .?'

'Yes? We're not getting any younger, are we?' he pointed out slyly.

'Precisely,' she agreed. 'We may have to put in a bit of overtime on that project.'

'Will your GP let you throw that little packet of pills away?'

'For a worthy cause like this, I'm sure of it.'

'And just when is this long evening supposed to end? Because I want to get on with that last task as soon as possible, you understand.'

'Oh, definitely!'

'So. . .?'

'Well, Gaye's hoping for extra donations tonight,' Megan sighed. 'She'd like to be able to announce that we've topped the 100,000 pound mark. I believe we'll need another 10,650 odd pounds, on top of what's been raised so far from ticket sales and other donations.'

'Let's hope it doesn't take too long,' he muttered, then dipped to trace the neckline of her dress with his lips once more.

The music stopped at that point and there was applause, followed by conversation, dessert and speeches—including Megan's.

'We haven't quite attained our goal for this evening, everyone,' she told the gathering, then flourished the pocket calculator Gaye had thrust into her hand. 'Any further donations will be tallied at once—'

She was forced into silence at this point as Gaye suddenly seized the microphone. 'And we won't start the dancing again until we hit the mark,' she threatened ominously, then quipped with a siren frown, 'Don't try to leave now, Nina and Richard. The doors have already been locked, and they're going to stay that way! We're now less than 3000 pounds short. Please be generous, all of you!'

Some endless minutes later, after an earnestly supportive speech from the mayor, an increasingly impatient

Callum suddenly discovered just how vital an MRI scanner was to the future of Camberton Hospital. With Megan's full support, signalled by a nod from her trapped position on the dais, he wrote out a very generous cheque.

'Let's go before Gaye decides we have to come up with the whole million,' he muttered as they finally reached the door.

'I'd raise it somehow, if I had to, to be alone with you,' she told him tenderly.

MILLS & BOON®

Medical Romance™

COMING NEXT MONTH

NOT HUSBAND MATERIAL! by Caroline Anderson
Audley Memorial Hospital

Jill Craig was not impressed when the flirtatious, but very handsome Zach Samuels breezed into the Audley and proceeded to charm everyone—including herself! She could not deny the intense desire that they both felt, but could she trust him to love only her?

A CAUTIOUS LOVING by Margaret O'Neill

Dr Thomas Brodie was reluctant to hire Miranda Gibbs. Why was such a beautiful, intelligent and diligent woman moving to the country? But then he saw her in action as a nurse. Miranda might get the job but she would never have his heart...

WINGS OF SPIRIT by Meredith Webber
Flying Doctors

Christa Cassimatis had known station owner Andrew Walsh on a strictly professional basis for months, so she was astonished when Andrew suddenly proposed! She barely knew the man, and now he wanted to get married! She knew it must be for all the wrong reasons...

PRESTON'S PRACTICE by Carol Wood

The name Preston Lynley rang alarm bells for Vanessa Perry! But then Preston provoked the most surprising reactions, including being incredibly attracted to him, from the minute she had begun her new job at his Medical Practice! But he also made Vanessa remember her tragic past—and his link to it...

MILLS & BOON®

Medical Romance™

Flying Doctors

Don't miss this exciting new mini-series from popular
Medical Romance author, Meredith Webber.

**Set in the heat of the Australian outback,
the Flying Doctor mini-series experiences
the thrills, drama and romance of life
on a flying doctor station.**

Look out for:

Wings of Spirit by Meredith Webber
in June '97

FOUR FREE
specially selected
Medical Romance™ novels
<u>PLUS</u> a FREE Mystery Gift
when you return this page...

Return this coupon and we'll send you 4 Medical Romance novels and a mystery gift absolutely FREE! We'll even pay the postage and packing for you.

We're making you this offer to introduce you to the benefits of the Reader Service™– FREE home delivery of brand-new Medical Romance novels, at least a month before they are available in the shops, FREE gifts and a monthly Newsletter packed with information, competitions, author profiles and lots more...

Accepting these FREE books and gift places you under no obligation to buy, you may cancel at any time, even after receiving just your free shipment. Simply complete the coupon below and send it to:

MILLS & BOON READER SERVICE, FREEPOST, CROYDON, SURREY, CR9 3WZ.

READERS IN EIRE PLEASE SEND COUPON TO PO BOX 4546, DUBLIN 24

NO STAMP NEEDED

Yes, please send me 4 free Medical Romance novels and a mystery gift. I understand that unless you hear from me, I will receive 4 superb new titles every month for just £2.20* each, postage and packing free. I am under no obligation to purchase any books and I may cancel or suspend my subscription at any time, but the free books and gift will be mine to keep in any case. (I am over 18 years of age)

M7XE

Ms/Mrs/Miss/Mr_____
BLOCK CAPS PLEASE
Address_____

_____

_____ Postcode _____